*If he wasn't careful, Ryan thought,
Julia's kiss could knock him
to his knees.*

"Perfect," she whispered in his ear. "Just perfect."

"Here," he murmured huskily, leaning toward her again, "let me show you what perfect really is."

She stopped him with her hand against his chest. "That's not necessary. She's gone."

"Who's gone?" he asked, confused.

"Well, my daughter was at the window. I wanted to make certain I looked as if I'd had a wonderful evening. That I was enjoying all the...extras a fourteen-year-old would expect when two adults go out on a date. I needed her to see that I was having a...good time." Then she added, "That's why I went out with you."

Her eyes raised to his, mortification exposed for him to see. Obviously she'd let something slip. And he meant to find out what.

Dear Reader,

This month, Silhouette Romance unveils our newest promotion, VIRGIN BRIDES. This series, which celebrates first love, will feature original titles by some of Romance's best-loved stars, starting with perennial favorite Diana Palmer. In *The Princess Bride,* a feisty debutante sets her marriage sights on a hard-bitten, cynical cowboy. At first King Marshall resists, but when he realizes he may lose this innocent beauty—forever—he finds himself doing the unthinkable: proposing.

Stranded together in a secluded cabin, single mom and marked woman Madison Delaney finds comfort—and love—in *In Care of the Sheriff,* this month's FABULOUS FATHERS title, as well as the first book of Susan Meier's new miniseries, TEXAS FAMILY TIES. Donna Clayton's miniseries MOTHER & CHILD also debuts with *The Stand-by Significant Other.* A workaholic businesswoman accepts her teenage daughter's challenge to "get a life," but she quickly discovers that safe—but irresistibly sexy—suitor Ryan Shane is playing havoc with her heart.

In Laura Anthony's compelling new title, *Bride of a Texas Trueblood,* Deannie Hollis would do *anything* to win back her family homestead—even marry the son of her enemy. In Elizabeth Harbison's sassy story, *Two Brothers and a Bride,* diner waitress Joleen Wheeler finds herself falling for the black-sheep brother of her soon-to-be fiancé.... Finally, Martha Shields tells a heartwarming tale about a woman's quest for a haven and the strong, silent rancher who shows her that *Home is Where Hank is.*

In April and May, look for VIRGIN BRIDES titles by Elizabeth August and Annette Broadrick. And enjoy each and every emotional, heartwarming story to be found in a Silhouette Romance.

Regards,

Joan Marlow Golan

Joan Marlow Golan
Senior Editor Silhouette Books

Please address questions and book requests to:
Silhouette Reader Service
U.S.: 3010 Walden Ave., P.O. Box 1325, Buffalo, NY 14269
Canadian: P.O. Box 609, Fort Erie, Ont. L2A 5X3

THE STAND-BY
SIGNIFICANT
OTHER

Donna Clayton

Silhouette
ROMANCE™
Published by Silhouette Books
America's Publisher of Contemporary Romance

This book is dedicated to Wanda White
My Aunt Sis
With lots of love

SILHOUETTE BOOKS

ISBN 0-373-19284-3

THE STAND-BY SIGNIFICANT OTHER

Copyright © 1998 by Donna Fasano

Printed in U.S.A.

Books by Donna Clayton

Silhouette Romance

Mountain Laurel #720
Taking Love in Stride #781
Return of the Runaway Bride #999
Wife for a While #1039
Nanny and the Professor #1066
Fortune's Bride #1118
Daddy Down the Aisle #1162
*Miss Maxwell Becomes a Mom #1211
*Nanny in the Nick of Time #1217
*Beauty and the Bachelor Dad #1223
†The Stand-By Significant Other #1284

*The Single Daddy Club
†Mother & Child

DONNA CLAYTON

is proud to be a recipient of the Holt Medallion, an award honoring outstanding literary talent. And seeing her work appear on the Waldenbooks series bestsellers list has given her a great deal of joy and satisfaction.

Reading is one of Donna's favorite ways to wile away a rainy afternoon. She loves to hike, too. Another hobby added to her list of fun things to do is traveling. She fell in love with Europe during her first trip abroad recently and plans to return often. Oh, and Donna still collects cookbooks, but as her writing career grows, she finds herself using them less and less.

Donna loves to hear from her readers. You can write her at P.O. Box 9785, Newark, DE 19714-9785.

Julia's Thoughts on Motherhood

Help! My fourteen-year-old daughter has been struck with a horrible malady. *Hormones!* Kelly has fallen for a boy and she's breaking all my parental rules to be with him. I can see that mothering this teen of mine is going to give me a headful of gray hair.

Haven't I tried to be a good role model? Don't I strive to be an independent woman, a good single parent? I was floored when my daughter used all these qualities against me. How could she say my life is dull, that I don't know how to have fun?

Looks like my teen is forcing me to bend a few of my own rules. And it seems these rules involve a man—a willing "significant other"—who can help me prove to Kelly that I'm not so dull after all.

I have complete control over this situation. I can handle my teenage daughter. I can handle having a man in my life (seeing that he's only going to be in my life for such a short time!) I *can* handle this...as long as I don't do something foolish...like fall in love.

Chapter One

Julia Jones took the left turn with just enough speed to make her tires cry out in complaint. Then she gripped the steering wheel as she barreled down the narrow, curving lane that would take her to her partner's big, rambling farmhouse. She was acutely conscious of the deserted county road, relieved, in fact, that she could take her aggression out on the pavement.

She'd been angry as a riled hornet when she'd left her Wilmington town house, stinging mad at Kelly, her teenage daughter. And it seemed the twenty-minute drive through the lush, rolling hills of Hockessin, Delaware hadn't lightened Julia's black mood one bit. She sure hoped Charlotte would have some of her famous chamomile tea waiting. But she doubted even the most potent herbal concoction her business partner could come up with could calm the dismay that had her head and her stomach churning. What she needed was a stiff shot of whiskey.

Teenagers! Sheesh, Julia thought, raising one was enough to turn a mother to alcohol.

The idea actually made one corner of her mouth curl, despite her dark mood. Charlotte would laugh at her, knowing Julia never touched anything stronger than an occasional glass of wine.

As she passed under the dense overhang of tree branches, unbidden images of Kelly flitted through her mind. Julia pictured her dark-haired daughter as she'd been in years past: in a layered tulle tutu twirling on-stage; with the proud offering of a handmade gift of brightly tinted noodles made into a necklace; in shiny patent-leather shoes on her first day of school.

When exactly had it been that ballet and piano lessons had become passé in her daughter's mind? So "uncool" as Kelly would say. Sighing wistfully, Julia wished she could go back to those days gone by when Kelly's gaze had been filled with nothing but adoration and love as the child had looked at her mother.

Julia drove around Charlotte's white farmhouse and parked near the kitchen door. Where had the years gone? Julia wondered. Time had flown by so quickly. And now Kelly was a teenager. A teenager who had begun making irrational demands.

Getting out of the car, Julia noticed that she felt trembly inside. She opened the trunk and lifted out the hefty case of Cornish hens. The party she and Charlotte were catering this evening was small, but as proud owners of Gold Ribbon Catering, both women were in agreement that their food would be fresh and delicious whether they served twenty-five people or two hundred and fifty.

Julia leaned back against the weight of the ungainly box as she made her way to the door. In just a moment she'd be standing in Charlotte's large kitchen, filling the cavities of these small birds with the special wild rice stuffing that had become a Gold Ribbon signature as she told her friend and partner all about her problems with Kelly.

Tactful Charlotte never took sides or gave advice when Julia discussed her difficulties with Kelly. But she was sure Charlotte would have something to say about this latest mother-daughter argument.

Dating, for goodness' sake. Dating *boys!* Quite frankly, the mere idea of her daughter going out alone with some strange boy made Julia shudder.

Wedging the heavy box against her hip and the door jamb, Julia freed one hand and knocked lightly on the glass windowpane.

Kelly was only fourteen years old. She was definitely too young to date. Julia had pointed out that fact, swiftly and unequivocally stamping out any notion in her daughter's head of going to the movies tonight with that boy. And the fact that Kelly had lamented that he was "just the cutest guy in the whole ninth grade" hadn't softened Julia's decision one bit. If anything, that tidbit of information had only strengthened her resolve. It was the "cute" ones a mother had to watch out for!

The Cornish hens slipped in her grasp, and Julia was forced to make a quick grab to keep them from falling to the ground. That's all she needed…to see two dozen tiny bird carcasses rolling around in the flower bed.

Where was Charlotte? These hens were getting heavier by the second.

Julia knocked again. This time with a little more force.

"Charlotte," she grumbled out loud, her tone complaining, "where are you?" She fumbled awkwardly in her tiny purse for her ring of keys and let herself inside the spacious kitchen.

Now groaning under the weight, Julia shuffled to the oak table and set down the box.

"Hey," she called, "is anybody home?"

The house was quiet. She gazed around at the honey-oak cabinets with their hand-painted porcelain handles. Julia loved this room. Loved this house. Charlotte had purchased it eighteen months ago using part of her divorce settlement as a down payment.

Julia had known Charlotte for years. As the sole owner of Gold Ribbon back then, she'd catered many of the dinner parties Charlotte had given for her husband, an affluent and well-known Wilmington businessman. And Charlotte's passion for cooking kept her in the kitchen much of the time during those parties.

After Charlotte's divorce, Julia had been stunned by the way the woman had picked herself up, dusted herself off and gotten on with life. Charlotte had approached her about a position at Gold Ribbon as a chef. Although she knew her friend had absolutely no head for business, Julia also realized that Charlotte's uncanny talent with food would be a definite asset to her catering company. But Gold Ribbon had been a small proprietorship, and the profits brought in by the business hadn't allowed for the salary of another chef. So Julia had had to turn Charlotte down.

Then Charlotte had made a surprising offer—she'd buy her way into Gold Ribbon. That's when Julia realized just how large Charlotte's divorce settlement had been.

Julia hadn't blinked an eye. She'd taken Charlotte up on her offer, knowing Gold Ribbon would profit, not only from Charlotte's culinary abilities, but also from the woman's huge resource of potential customers—all those friends she'd made while being married to that affluent businessman. Now she and Charlotte had more catering jobs than they could handle. Julia took care of the business end of things—advertising, scheduling parties, billing, ordering and buying supplies—while Charlotte stuck to what she did best: slicing, dicing, baking, simmering…anything that had to do with food preparation.

Their partnership had turned out to be successful. Extremely so. Charlotte had become more than a partner, though. She'd become Julia's best friend.

The sound of water running in the upper regions of the house caught Julia's attention.

What the heck was Charlotte doing taking a shower at one o'clock in the afternoon? A frown bit into Julia's brow as she looked toward the back staircase. She was certain Charlotte expected her. They'd talked on the phone just yesterday afternoon. Didn't Charlotte realize they had hens to stuff? Green beans to snap? Vichyssoise to prepare?

She went to the refrigerator and pulled open the door. Thank goodness the wild rice stuffing was ready and waiting. Julia reached for the large stainless-steel bowl.

A teakettle began to whistle, jerking Julia's attention to the stove behind her. Leaving the bowl of stuffing where it sat, she automatically crossed the room and turned off the gas flame.

"What are you trying to do, Charlotte," she whispered under her breath, "burn down your beautiful house?"

Julia heard the shower cut off suddenly. There was a loud thumping of feet as Charlotte raced across the bathroom floor. Julia bit back a smile. Her friend must have remembered the teakettle and was hurrying to check on the boiling water.

Charlotte *was* absentminded, but the woman always remembered. A little late sometimes, but she always remembered. Julia had learned to work around Charlotte's scattered thinking, a good example being yesterday's phone call to remind her partner of tonight's catering appointment and their one o'clock meeting to prepare the meal.

Cocking her head, Julia felt there was something...strange about the sound of those footfalls, though. She shook her head, trying to figure it out. Somehow they sounded heavy. Much more solid than they should have.

Her gaze swiveled toward the stairs, and it seemed that time slowed to a near halt. Bare, muscular calves came into view. Julia's eyes grew large when she saw the knees and steel-like thighs.

If those were Charlotte's legs—Julia's gaze widened even more—then the woman had decided to make some sort of hairy, primeval fashion statement.

Julia was so taken aback by the sight of the towel-clad man that she couldn't speak, couldn't move. And he was in such a rush to get to the kitchen that he didn't even see her standing there by the stove until he was in the middle of the room. Her presence brought him to a sudden, startled halt.

His mouth parted, but no words passed his lips. A tiny, intriguing crease appeared between his tawny eyebrows. His blue eyes blinked once, twice.

Gee, had she ever seen eyes that blue? And that face. Men this attractive usually graced the covers of glossy fashion magazines.

The unbidden thoughts momentarily sidetracked the mute-inducing surprise that had walloped her like a swift uppercut to the jaw. One corner of her mouth ticked upward in the smallest of appreciative grins. If he were to appear on the cover of any magazine, her admiring musings silently continued, he'd have to wear something a little less...revealing.

Her eyes blazed a purely spontaneous path down the length of his body. Crystal droplets of water clung to his smooth neck and broad shoulders; the rivulets cascading down his tanned skin were evidence of how quickly he'd exited the shower. His well-formed pectorals glistened with damp, golden curls. Mesmerized now, her gaze followed the satiny hair as it tapered into a vee just above his taut stomach. She simply couldn't resist taking a quick peek at his well-defined abdominal muscles. This man obviously took excellent care of his body.

The fluffy white towel that was wrapped around his waist exposed a healthy slice of muscular thigh, and before she realized it, she found herself staring at his nicely shaped feet.

He shifted his weight and suddenly Julia returned to her senses, realizing the blatant manner in which she'd appraised this...this...complete stranger. She swallowed, her gaze flying to his face as she felt her cheeks suffuse with heat.

One full brow was quirked upward, and his blue eyes held an unreadable expression that for some reason only served to heighten Julia's embarrassment.

And for the span of one quick heartbeat, she wondered if she should feel endangered by the nearly naked man who stood in the middle of Charlotte's kitchen. But the thought didn't last long, because for some reason it seemed unimaginable that he might threaten her in any way. The vibrations she sensed emanating from him had nothing to do with danger. What she did perceive, though, was his bewilderment regarding who she was and what she was doing here.

Well, those exact questions were rolling around in her mind, too.

It seemed that many long minutes had passed since the teakettle had whistled and the man had rushed into the room. Julia knew, however, that everything had happened within the ticking of just a few short seconds.

Say something, darn it, she silently commanded. *The longer you stand here gawking, the longer you look like a complete and total idiot.*

Ryan's head was swimming with questions. Who was this dark-haired beauty who had invaded Charlotte's home? What was she doing here? How did she get into the house? And what did she think she was doing sizing him up like she was half starved and he was a prime piece of sirloin just waiting to be seasoned and grilled over hot coals?

Well…he really didn't mind the way her onyx eyes had trailed lazily down his body; however, he would have liked there to be a little more between him and her scrutiny besides the not-quite-large-enough bath towel tucked around his midriff.

He hadn't taken his eyes off the woman's face since he'd barged into the room suddenly realizing he wasn't alone. His eyes narrowed as he studied her. He still couldn't quite believe she was standing there. He just wished he could gather his wits enough to put two words together.

"Hi."

Her tiny greeting sounded stentorian in the silent and awkward confusion that had enveloped the kitchen. And because he could think of nothing else to say, he lifted his hand lamely and parroted, ''Hi.''

''I, uh, I took the teakettle off the burner.'' She indicated the stove behind her with a tiny tilt of her head.

In keeping with this totally farcical situation, he simply nodded his head. ''Thanks,'' he said, his tone ludicrously amiable.

The silence that followed was stiff, to say the least. The air became so strained that, for the first time since charging into the room, he averted his gaze from her face.

He glanced toward the big bay window, barely noting the profusion of color created by the flowers in the side garden. The surprise that had him dumbfounded was understandable. Yet for some strange reason he also felt...intrusive. Almost as if *he* was the one invading the house. As if *he* was the one who should apologize and explain. For the life of him he couldn't figure out the feelings. They were ridiculous, really. Hell, this whole predicament was ridiculous.

At long last, nerve impulses finally connected, sending his curious questions zooming toward the part of his brain that controlled his sense of speech.

''Who *are* you?'' he asked, the bewilderment he felt clearly obvious in the astonishment expressed in his voice.

As a lawyer, Ryan routinely questioned people on the witness stand. This situation had him feeling so...*weird*, like his inquiry was way out of line.

She blinked those coal-black eyes of hers, her dark lashes fanning against her sun-bronzed skin. Gazing at him, she took a moment to swallow and then said, ''I'm Julia Jones,'' as if that would explain everything.

The husky tone of her whisper caressed his ears and

he found the sound of it more than a little sexy. Her tongue darted across the length of her full bottom lip, a sight that nearly short-circuited Ryan's thinking. This woman was so attractive, so appealing.

He'd met lots of women who made a conscious effort to use their feminine wiles to their best advantage. But the sensuality exuded by the woman standing in Charlotte's kitchen was in no way forced or calculated, and Ryan found the completely natural manner in which she batted her dark lashes, moistened her luscious lips, to be downright erotic.

"And you are?" she softly prompted.

"Ryan Shane," he said without hesitation. "I'm Charlotte's cousin."

"Ah." Julia Jones nodded. "Charlotte's cousin." Almost as an afterthought she added, "It's strange she didn't mention she had family coming to visit."

Ryan was about to speak when the sexy sound of Julia's laughter cut his intended words right off the tip of his tongue.

"Actually," she said softly, almost to herself, "it's not."

His brow furrowed with momentary confusion. "It's not what?" he asked.

"It's not strange that she didn't mention your visit to me," Julia explained, her beautiful face softening. "It probably slipped her mind."

Her dark eyes gleamed with humor, and Ryan's heart thumped against his rib cage. No two ways about it, this woman was just adorable.

"Charlotte did forget, didn't she?" Julia asked.

Ryan nodded. "Yeah. I arrived last night. And when she answered the door, her face registered complete and utter surprise." He chuckled as he remembered. "But I must admit, she recovered quickly."

The smile on Julia's face widened. "She always does. That's Charlotte all over." With barely a pause, she went on. "Welcome to Wilmington. How long will you be staying?"

"Well, actually," he said, "I've moved in."

The instant of surprise expressed in her eyes was quickly suppressed.

"Charlotte invited me," he rushed to assure her.

Why did he feel the need to assure this woman of anything? he wondered. Other than her name, he knew nothing about her. Nonetheless, he had this overwhelming urge to justify his presence in his cousin's house.

"And I don't plan to stay long. Only until I can find my own place."

"Oh," was all she said.

Then her gaze swept toward the staircase and back to his face. "So," she said, her tone tinged with hope, "is she here?"

"Well, no," he said. "We stayed up late last night talking. So we both slept in. Charlotte went out to buy bagels and some cream cheese for breakfast."

"Don't you mean *brunch?*"

The touch of light sarcasm in her voice wasn't lost on him, but Ryan didn't allow it to affect him. He and Charlotte had deserved to catch up.

He smiled easily. "I guess that is what I mean."

Julia Jones groaned long and loud, throwing her hands into the air. "Oh, Charlotte. We have birds to stuff. How could you have forgotten that we have a dinner party to cater tonight?"

"Ah," Ryan remarked as this piece of the puzzle snapped into place, "so you're the business partner."

Julia's weary gaze settled on him. "I'm the partner."

Her long-suffering tone made him grin. "I feel for you. Running a business with Charlotte can't be easy. Ever since I can remember, my cousin's been...how can I put this delicately? A little scatterbrained?"

"But she's got a good heart."

His smile broadened. It was nice to hear Julia coming to Charlotte's immediate defense.

"And can that woman cook," she continued, her tone filled with obvious admiration. Then she shrugged. "So I put up with her tiny...shortcoming. I'm sure I have a flaw or two of my own."

From what Ryan had witnessed, Julia Jones looked damned near perfect in every respect. But he figured voicing that opinion, in his present state of undress, wouldn't receive a very good reaction from the woman, so he simply kept the thought to himself.

"Okay," Julia whispered, "looks like our tight schedule just got a little tighter."

There wasn't a trace of panic in her voice, Ryan recognized, just a cool, calm efficiency. But that didn't keep him from wanting to reach out to her, and although he hated to admit it, he highly suspected his underlying motivation was wrapped up in how attractive he found her.

"I can help," he offered, cringing at the eagerness in his words.

She cut her eyes at him. "Not dressed like that, you can't."

"What?" He lifted his hands, palms up, feigning great insult. "Are you saying that near nakedness and food preparation don't mix?"

Her laughter was instant and spontaneous as his outrageous question caught her off guard. Hearing the blatantly sexy sound of it, Ryan felt the blood pulse through his body a little quicker.

"Absolutely," she said once she'd gotten herself under control. "That's *exactly* what I'm saying."

Merriment danced a jig all around them for a quick, silent moment, and for the span of two full heartbeats, Ryan felt as if he'd connected with Julia Jones.

The back door slammed open and Charlotte entered the kitchen in a frenzied whirlwind of panic. "I remembered, Julia. I'm here. I was…" She paused, looking from her partner to Ryan, and then back again. "Paying for…"

Finally her words trailed off into oblivion as she took a second glance at Ryan. Her gaze fell to his towel-clad midriff. When her brown eyes lifted to his face, there was mischief brewing there.

"Well, Julia," Charlotte said, keeping her attention riveted to Ryan, "I see you've met my cousin." Her mouth quirked upward as she added, "Almost *all* of him, in fact."

Ryan felt mortified. And his self-conscious glance at Julia told him she was just as flustered and disconcerted as he.

Their eyes locked and held, both of them looking as guilty as sin. Like teenagers who had gotten caught necking in the back seat of a car on a hot and sultry Saturday night. Julia's gaze slid away from his.

Seemingly out of nowhere the aroma of warm, freshly baked bagels wafted through the air. Too bad this wacky situation had stolen his appetite.

Simultaneously he and Julia turned to Charlotte.

"The teakettle was on the burner," Julia said, as if that simple explanation would absolve the two of them of any and all perceived wrong-doing.

"Yeah," Ryan added, cringing at the defensiveness in his tone. "I just now jumped out of the shower to turn off the stove."

As if to prove his point, he wiped his hand across his chest expecting it to come away wet.

Bone dry. He darted a look at his palm. Gee, just how long had he been standing here half naked?

The same question was written all over Charlotte's amused expression.

He wasn't going to explain himself to his cousin. He was a grown man. He didn't need to account for every moment of his time to anyone.

Why, then, was he experiencing this odd urge to lower his gaze? To scuff his foot on the floor? To slink off upstairs?

Lifting his chin, he leveled his gaze on his cousin, determined to leave the room with some dignity.

"I, uh, I—" He snapped his jaw shut. This sudden nervous speech impediment infuriated him.

Narrowing his eyes, he glared at Charlotte. "I'm going to go get dressed, damn it!" And he turned on his bare heel and stalked from the room.

"Well, now…"

Julia heard the teasing quality in Charlotte's voice, saw the animated manner in which her partner sauntered further into the room, and knew she was in deep trouble.

Charlotte put the bag of bagels on the counter as she lamented, "There I was racing down the road, feeling horrible that you'd have to start the preparations for tonight's party all by your lonesome self."

"Look, Char—"

"And here all the time," she continued, "you had a

big, strapping man to carry in your case of Cornish hens. I should never have worried.''

"Ryan did *not* carry in the hens," Julia informed Charlotte.

The sparkling glint in her partner's eyes convinced Julia that the good-natured teasing wasn't quite over yet.

Charlotte reached into the bag and pulled out a chewy bagel. "Why, I could have had an accident out there in all that traffic." She nibbled at the bread, not even bothering to suppress her grin.

Julia plunked her fist on her hip. "Those roads were deserted out there. I drove them to get here, remember? And I've never known you to drive over the speed limit." Now it was Julia's turn to joke. "To the contrary..." Her grin now matched Charlotte's. "You drive like an overcautious, old—"

"Now, now," Charlotte warned, wagging her index finger in Julia's general direction. "Let's not start calling names."

Sighing, Julia relented. "You're right. We've got too much work to do." She marched past Charlotte and began fussing to get the carton of hens open. "Grab that bowl of stuffing from the fridge."

"Sure thing," Charlotte said, going to the refrigerator. "But don't think you're going to get out of telling me what you think of my gorgeous cousin."

Ryan Shane was the last topic of conversation she wanted to get involved in. She still couldn't quite believe how she'd reacted to the man's handsome face, his rock-hard body. Not to mention his boyish charm. Sheesh, Julia thought, with that purely male charisma of his, Ryan Shane could probably coax the moon down from the sky. But she certainly wouldn't admit to that opinion...even to her best friend.

"He's, ah, nice."

Julia felt smug that she'd come up with the perfect compliment. Middle-of-the-road positive without being too flattering.

"Nice?" Charlotte whirled around to face her. "He might be my cousin, but that doesn't mean I can't tell the truth. That man is..." She searched the air for an appropriate adjective. "Gorgeous."

Julia gritted her teeth. "You said that already. Can we start stuffing these birds? We have a lot to do in the next five hours."

"Okay, okay," Charlotte muttered, turning to the sink to wash her hands. "Besides, I might as well not even *think* of anything happening between the two of you."

The statement had Julia's hand freezing on the cardboard box, her nerves jangling through her body.

"Seems that my wonderful cousin is just as much against relationships as you are."

Forcing herself not to look at Charlotte, Julia kept her gaze glued to the plastic that lined the box of Cornish hens. She held her breath, willing Charlotte to explain herself.

Finally, Julia was forced to either take a breath or fall over in a dead faint. Inhaling was the better choice. It looked as though she'd get no more information regarding Ryan Shane from Charlotte. Unless she asked, of course. And Julia would rather die a slow and painful death than do that.

It was enough to know that the man wasn't interested in getting involved. At least that's what Charlotte had implied. And that was perfect. Because neither was she.

A woman didn't need a man to be happy. Or successful. She'd learned that the hard way.

Taking a covert glance at Charlotte, Julia watched her

pull leeks and potatoes, cream and yogurt from the fridge for the creamy chilled soup they planned to prepare for tonight. Clearly, Charlotte's flighty mind was no longer thinking of Ryan, and Julia was annoyed at herself for feeling disappointed.

"So," Charlotte said from across the kitchen, "how's Miss Kelly today? And how come she didn't come to lend us a hand?"

At the mention of her daughter's name, Julia felt as though she'd been struck by a solid wall of pure emotion: anger, frustration, fear. It tumbled over her, making her feel the need to gasp for breath.

"What is it, Julia?" Charlotte asked. "What's wrong?"

"Oh, Charlotte." The simple presence of her friend's sympathetic ear brought tears to Julia's eyes. "You won't believe what Kelly wants to do."

Chapter Two

Julia slipped the key into the lock of her front door, feeling that the evening had been a great success.

The food she and Charlotte had prepared had turned out exceptionally well. So well, in fact, that when the hostess had come into the kitchen to sample the various dishes, she'd oohed and aahed, smacked her lips and promised that Gold Ribbon would receive a big, fat tip when the final installment of the bill was paid.

Glancing at her watch, Julia saw that it was nearly nine fifteen. Good, she was early.

After she and Charlotte had delivered the meal to their client, they had celebrated by stopping for a burger and a thick vanilla milk shake. They'd sat in the restaurant and gabbed about all sorts of topics. It wasn't something they did often, but Julia had been thankful for the opportunity to talk more with Charlotte. Actually, Julia had been thankful for the opportunity to avoid for a little longer the trying task of facing Kelly.

When Julia had called home to tell her daughter she

was having dinner with Charlotte and she'd be late, Kelly's refusal to pick up the phone had annoyed Julia. But she'd simply left a message of when she'd be home and what her daughter might fix herself to eat, certain Kelly was standing there listening to every word.

At the restaurant Charlotte had listened as Julia complained bitterly about Kelly's hormone rush and sudden awareness of the opposite sex. Julia guessed she may have reacted a little unkindly when her friend had tried to point out that this "boy crazy" phase was a natural part of being a teen. But Julia simply hadn't wanted to hear it.

Although she was bound and determined not to be the kind of parent her own father had been, she was also determined to protect Kelly from her own stupidity. Mistakes made during adolescence could last a lifetime, and Julia had resolved long ago that the past wouldn't be repeated. Not with *her* daughter.

Muted rock music floated down from the upper regions of the house, letting Julia know Kelly was holed up in her room. Heaving a weary sigh, Julia mounted the stairs, unfastening the buttons of her blouse as she went. What she needed was a long soak in a hot bath.

Midway down the hall, she stopped at the closed bedroom door of Kelly's room. The pink notepaper taped at eye level had angry-looking, block-styled letters scrawled across it: Leave Me Alone.

She turned away from the door. Turned away from all the anger and stifled communication it symbolized. As she walked into her room, she shrugged off her blouse and then tossed it on the bed. Julia slipped out of her shoes and pulled off her trousers. She grabbed her robe and the novel sitting on her nightstand, and went back down the hall and into the bathroom she shared with

Kelly, keeping her eyes averted from the note plastered to her daughter's door.

Turning on the faucet, she adjusted the water temperature and then went to pull down a fresh towel from the linen shelf. After slipping out of her panties and bra, she stepped into the tub. Leaning her head against the cool enamel, she closed her eyes and waited for the warm, silky water to rise over her body.

When she turned off the faucet, the water dripped once or twice, and then all was silent. Well…almost silent. The muffled sound of Kelly's music permeated even the closed bathroom door, but Julia didn't have too much trouble blocking it out. As the mother of a rock-loving teen, she'd had plenty of practice doing just that.

Chapter Seven of the romance novel Julia was reading had the hero and heroine feeling frisky and full of sensual fun. She allowed herself to become lost in the quirky banter and sexual sparks this imaginary man and woman spurred in one another.

Slowly the tone of the book made a subtle change that focused less on fun and more on sensual pleasure. The images the talented author painted became more heated, more intense.

His lips burned a scalding trail down her neck, Julia read, *and a soft moan escaped from deep in her throat. He reached up and cupped her breast in his palm…*

Julia placed the book on the edge of the tub and sank deeper into the heated water. Closing her eyes, she slowly drew her fingertips down the length of her throat. A sharp, unbidden image of Ryan Shane appeared in her mind. But his sapphire gaze was so…different. So full of…passion. For her.

An audible sigh escaped her lips and she shifted her

weight in the tub. Water lapped at her breasts, and she felt her damp nipples bud in the cool air.

What would it feel like to be kissed by a man as handsome as Ryan? she wondered. His body had looked rock-hard and she couldn't help but ponder what his firm muscles would feel like under her fingertips. She shouldn't allow herself to wonder such things. But the sultry heat of the water had her feeling languid, and the sexy novel had stirred the most carnal portion of her imagination.

What did it matter if she fantasized? She knew there was no place for a man in her life. But that didn't mean she was any less human. Any less a woman. What harm could a little daydreaming do? Or should she call this *night*dreaming? The sky was dark, after all, she thought, the silent musings tugging her mouth into a tiny grin.

Lifting her hand from the water, she smoothed one hot, wet index finger across her bottom lip and allowed the sexy scenario to continue.

Ryan's mouth burned a scalding trail along her jaw. His hands smoothed over her abdomen. Julia felt her heart flutter under her rib cage, and her nipples drew even tighter. With her head reclined, her eyes closed, she arched her spine, easily imagining him kissing her lips, her chin, her throat, her shoulder. He hovered over her breasts, a hungry fire burning in his eyes. He lowered his mouth. His lips parted, his tongue darting out to—

Julia's eyes opened wide and she sat up with a suddenness that caused water to splash over the side of the tub. Her heart hammered, her breathing came in gasps.

The image had been so clear. Breathtakingly realistic. Frighteningly vivid. She'd almost been able to actually feel his lips on hers, his hands on her body, his tongue on her skin.

She shook her head, wiping the picture from her mind. Fantasizing about Ryan Shane had been a mistake. Seeing him today in all his bare-chested glory had chiseled his image in her brain a little too clearly.

Kelly's music floated into the room, and Julia locked onto it with every nuance of her concentration in an effort to remove Ryan from her thoughts. Her brow furrowed as she listened to the tune. She'd already heard that particular song since she'd been home.

The relaxing effect of the bath had disappeared, and Julia felt her neck and shoulders tense. She stood, reached for the towel and dried herself off.

Slipping into her robe, she let the water out of the tub and then opened the bathroom door. She had intended on going straight to bed, but lying in the darkness wasn't something she could face right now. Kelly's door, with that annoyingly demanding message posted on it, drew her like a magnet. She needed a diversion.

You'll only start another argument, Julia silently warned herself.

"Tough," she whispered out loud, and she knocked softly on the six paneled door. Besides, if she acted like the calm, sensible adult she was, Julia was certain she just might be able to make her daughter understand how she felt.

When her knock received no reply, she called, "Kelly?"

The only sound coming from the room was the raspy voice of a singer lamenting the awful state of the world.

"Come on, Kell," she said firmly. "Open up. I want to talk."

She tried turning the doorknob and wasn't surprised to find it locked.

"Kelly?" Her tone softened. "I know you're angry

about my not letting you go to the movies. But things aren't going to get any better unless we talk. We need to communicate, honey.''

Communication was important. Something Julia had never had with her father. And that's why she was bound and determined to keep the lines of verbal interaction wide open between herself and her daughter.

"Please, Kell," she said. "Let me in."

Again, no sounds of movement, only the twang of an electric guitar, the loud beat of drums.

Kelly's stubbornness sparked a flash of irritation in Julia.

"Don't you think for a minute," she said, "that I believe you're sleeping in there. Because I know you. I know you wouldn't miss 'Letterman' for the world."

She suddenly chuckled softly, her annoyance forgotten, as she added, "Well, you'd never miss his show if it wasn't for me making you hit the sack at a decent hour." Again, she knocked. "Kelly, honey, open the door."

Crossing her arms, she leaned against the jamb and thought over her next plan of action. Kelly's stubborn streak went deep, but then, the child came by it honestly. Julia could be just as stubborn.

Reaching up to the narrow ledge created by the door molding, she retrieved the small key. "I'm coming in," she announced, working the key into the tiny hole in the doorknob.

The door swung open. Bright moonlight filtered through the filmy curtains, giving the room a soft, lucent glow by which Julia could easily see the mounded coverlet of Kelly's bed.

Julia took a step toward the shadowy, prone form.

However, before she reached the bed, the curtains ruffled lightly in the warm summer breeze.

"Kelly," Julia chided automatically, "the air conditioner is on. Why would you open the window?"

Irritation swept through her as she moved to close the window. "What if I made you pay the next electric bill, young lady?" she asked, reaching behind the curtains. "Then maybe you'd care whether or not we're cooling the entire city block."

Something wasn't right, Julia thought. When she reached for the window sash, her knuckles should have grazed the screen.

"What…"

The question died on her lips when she saw that the screen had been removed from the window and propped against the wall. Julia flipped back the curtains and looked out the window.

A ladder! The extension ladder was leaning against the back of the house. Julia's heart leaped up into her throat, and she ran to the bed, throwing back the covers.

Pillows. Three of them stacked end to end. The blanket had been tucked over top of them. Kelly was gone. She'd left the house after Julia had forbidden her to do so.

After a moment of silence another song began to spew from the speakers, the CD player having obviously been programmed for continuous replay. But Julia's ears were deaf to the screeching instruments as she worried about Kelly.

With trembling fingers, Julia picked up the soft Raggedy Ann doll that always sat on the lacy coverlet of Kelly's bed. Hugging it to her chest, Julia knew in her bruised heart that her relationship with her daughter would never be the same again.

* * *

Julia sat in the darkness of Kelly's bedroom for over an hour, her mind racing a mile a minute on the chaotic track called parental concern. The straight-backed, wooden desk chair was beyond uncomfortable, but she was grateful for the agony that kept her wide awake.

She'd experienced a few moments of sheer panic when the phrase "teenage runaway" had flitted through her anguished brain. The idea of Kelly roaming the city streets alone and vulnerable was terrifying.

However, the signs had been quite clear that her daughter had every intention of returning tonight. Because Julia hadn't been home, there had been no reason for Kelly to leave through the window. The front door would have proved a much easier exit. The ladder propped up against the house and the locked bedroom door were evidence that Kelly had taken pains to devise a plan of reentry. Well, tonight there was one teenage girl who would learn just what happened to the best laid plans.

What bothered Julia the most was the fact that Kelly was being so deceptive. Her daughter's rebellion was being carried out in secret. On the sly. Julia was discovering that Kelly could be...sneaky. And that revelation sat in Julia's stomach like a cold, hard cement block.

The metallic creaking sound that came from outside the window alerted Julia that her daughter was home. The ladder scraped against the wooden sash, and Julia had to force herself not to move from the chair. Kelly was agile and athletic, Julia told herself. She was safe. She'd climbed that ladder plenty of times when they had painted the exterior of the house together.

A dark form cast a slow, unwieldy shadow against the

window shade. Across the room, Julia watched as Kelly placed her foot on the narrow ledge.

"Ooo," Kelly whispered frantically, her free hand reaching into the darkness for something, anything, to grasp for balance. Her arm became entangled in the sheer curtain, and she finally pitched forward, somersaulting onto the floor with a muffled, "Ooof!"

Julia marveled that the curtain, rod, shade and all hadn't come tumbling down on top of Kelly. The child's forceful exhalation told Julia that Kelly's knees and elbows would be bruised and sore tomorrow.

Good! Julia thought. Kelly deserved a few days of discomfort for what she'd done tonight.

The magnitude of the anger simmering low in her belly surprised Julia. Never before in her life had she ever wished pain on anyone, least of all her own daughter. She loved Kelly. But Julia felt hurt. And betrayed. By the one person she thought she could always trust.

Well, that trust was broken now.

Kelly had picked herself up off the floor. She stood in the darkness, heaved a sigh and then sat on the edge of the bed.

Julia reached over and snapped on the desk lamp.

"Mom!" Kelly's face paled. "What are you doin' home?"

For a moment Julia was silent. Then she said, "So you *did* get my message."

The teenager averted her gaze. "Sure," Kelly said, her tone tight with nerves. "You said you'd be home at ten."

"I said I'd be home *before* ten," Julia corrected.

Kelly stared at the corner of the room.

"Look at me, Kelly," Julia said. When her daughter's

dark eyes finally lifted to hers, Julia asked, "Where have you been?"

"Oh, well..." She bent her head, her gaze darting to the dresser, the floor, a picture on the wall. "I know you said not to go out. But, uh...Sheila, um, had a problem."

Then something extraordinary happened; Kelly shot her mother a defiant look. "Where've *you* been?"

Julia's smoldering anger flared, the heat of the flames forcing her to cross her arms over her chest. "Listen, young lady. I'm the parent here. I'll ask the questions."

"But, Mom—"

"Quiet!" Julia could feel herself trembling inside. "You had strict instructions not to leave this house. I want to know where you've been, and I want to know now."

The silence in the room seemed full of invisible movement as angry emotion snapped and sparked and spun in the dense air. Julia watched the muscles of her daughter's throat convulse as Kelly swallowed nervously.

"I told you," Kelly said. "I went to Sheila's."

The lie sliced through Julia's heart like a sharp knife. If Kelly had gone over to her best friend's house, then why the ladder, why the pillows under the coverlet, why the locked bedroom door? She would not cry, damn it! She was too furious for tears. The knot in Julia's throat ached as she stared at her daughter.

"Sheila needed to talk," Kelly went on, her words rushing out one after the other. "She broke up with her boyfriend today and, um...and she needed to tell me what happened."

Julia's continued silence seemed to urge Kelly on.

"You see..." The teenager's eyes grew larger as she built up the fabrication. "I talked to Sheila before you called. And she was cryin' and stuff. And then after you left your message, I decided you wouldn't mind if I went over there." Kelly blinked. And swallowed. "You know...to talk to her. To make her feel better."

The fact that her daughter was lying was as clear as the most expensive crystal. How was she to react? Julia wondered. As a single mom, she'd never experienced anything like this before. What was she supposed to say to Kelly?

In a flash, Julia journeyed back in time to a painful place full of bitterness and humiliation, full of angry frustration. "You're only heaping coals of fire and damnation on your shoulders," she could hear her father shout, his face red and contorted with rage.

"Heaping fire and...what?"

Kelly's bewildered question snapped Julia back to the present. She hadn't thought of specific instances in her horrible childhood in ages. Had she really murmured those words aloud? Dear Lord, she had to get control of herself. She didn't want anger to cause her to do things she might regret. To say things that would make Kelly hate her.

"Look, Kelly..." Hearing the quiver in her voice, she stopped, cleared her throat and started again. "Look, I know you're lying. I'm your mom. I know when you're not telling the truth. Besides—" she shook her head "—you don't lie well."

Julia pressed her lips together and uncrossed her arms in an effort to relax. "I know you didn't go to Sheila's. Now, we can play all sorts of games designed to get you to tell the truth about where you went and who you were with. But I think it would be best if you just tell me the truth." She closed her eyes a moment, then sighing heavily, she directed her gaze at Kelly. "Although I'm pretty sure I know where you went."

Kelly's nervous countenance was taken over by a fierce and sudden stubbornness. "If you know where I was," she said softly, "then I don't need to tell you, do I?"

Julia didn't move. How dare she act so flippant! Kelly's impertinent attitude ignited a furious fire in Julia that was so hot it burned out of control.

"I want that boy's name," Julia demanded. "I want to ask his parents what they think of him helping a four-teen-year-old girl sneak out of the house."

"I did not sneak out," Kelly shouted childishly. "I only sneaked in!"

"I will not argue semantics with you, Kelly. I want that boy's name. I'm going to call his parents right now—"

"You can't do that!" Her daughter's eyes widened in horror.

"I can," she said. "And I will."

"B-but, Mom..."

The frantic tears welling in Kelly's eyes didn't soften Julia's angry determination one bit.

"He'll tell everyone!" Kelly reached out unwittingly and snatched the stuffed doll to her chest. "Everyone will know! They'll laugh at me."

"That won't really matter, will it?" Julia snapped. "Since you'll be spending the rest of your life staring at these four walls."

"Ground me. Go ahead. I don't care. But you can't call Tyler's parents." There was pleading in Kelly's dark eyes. "Everyone will talk about me."

Julia's jaw tightened. "You should have thought about that before you lied and plotted and schemed." Her anger was now in full control of her tongue. "You should be ashamed. Sneaking out in the night like a common little—''

Through the scarlet fog in her brain, Julia realized those weren't her words tumbling from her lips. Thank goodness she'd clamped her trembling hand over her mouth. These weren't her thoughts and opinions stamping around in her head. They belonged to *him*. Words and phrases meant to humiliate and degrade. She never wanted Kelly to feel demeaned and shameful the way she herself had been made to feel.

Sliding her hand from her face, she inhaled shakily. "I'm sorry." The apology sounded rough, as if her throat was lined with gritty sandpaper. "I think it would be best if…if we talked about this tomorrow. We both need to calm down."

She turned toward the door.

"No!"

Aghast at her daughter's sharp tone, Julia's chin tipped up and she looked into Kelly's tear-streaked face.

"I want to talk now!" Kelly said. "Right now. What did I do that was so wrong?"

The teenager's words seemed wrenched right from the heart, but the terrific surge of anger had taken such a toll on Julia that all she could feel was a limp numbness.

"I went to the movies," Kelly cried. "That's all. I even went to the early show so I could get in before you."

Julia's voice was flat as she responded. "You went to the movies with that boy. After I forbade you to go. You broke the rules, Kelly." Her tone lowered an octave. "You broke the rules."

"What do you want from me?"

The question her daughter hurled at her was overflowing with tearful anguish, and Julia felt her heart stir with something akin to compassion. But she refused to give in.

"I want you to be honest," Julia said. "I want to know that, when I leave you at home alone, that's where you'll be. I want to know I can trust you. I want you to do the right thing. I want you to follow the rules."

"Rules, rules, rules!" Kelly shoved the doll away from her. "You don't want me to have any fun. You want me to be a little clone of you!"

A frown bit into Julia's brow. "What is that supposed to mean?"

"You work twelve hours a day, seven days a week," Kelly said. "If you're not cooking for someone, you're out shopping for supplies or pressing someone for advertising. You never go out for fun. We never *do* anything together."

"How can you say that?" Julia shook her head in genuine bewilderment. "We do things together."

"Like what?" Kelly challenged, her overwrought emotions forcing up the volume of her voice. "Cook? We bake cheesecakes, and cookies with weird fillings. We experiment new side dishes with strange vegetables. And we make whole wheat rolls. All for other people. You call that fun?"

It was true that Julia loved to cook, loved to shop. Building Gold Ribbon into a successful business was exhilarating. Didn't Kelly understand that?

"How can you make rules for me? You don't have fun. You don't have friends. You never go out. How can you tell me how to live my life when you don't even have a life of your own?"

Julia's frown deepened, unable to name the emotion roiling deep in her gut.

"Gold Ribbon *isn't* a life!" Kelly yelled. "I don't

want to be like you. All you do is work. You're dull. Your life is dull. I won't follow your stupid rules. I won't! Not when you don't even know how to...not until you can...not when..." Kelly's frustration finally got the best of her. "I just won't, damn it!"

Staring into her daughter's gaze, Julia listened as Kelly described an existence full of drudgery and toil. That's the life Kelly thought her mother lived. Obviously.

Suddenly, Julia realized what she was feeling. Insulted. Scorned. Belittled. By her own daughter.

Her eyes might be dry, but the pain that broke her heart into a thousand jagged shards was almost more than she could bare. There was nothing Julia could think to do...except leave the room. And close the door softly behind her.

"What you *need,* Ryan," Charlotte said over coffee on Thursday morning, "is a woman."

The chaos—and yes, he'd admit it, the sheer panic—that had continued to run rampant though his brain since Monday didn't keep him from looking at his cousin as though a second head had suddenly sprouted from her shoulders.

"Are you kidding me?" The question dripped with incredulity. "It's a woman I'm trying to avoid."

"Don't I know it," Charlotte muttered. "You've been avoiding women for as long as I can remember."

Ryan couldn't help but toss her a grin that was full of self-defense. "That's not entirely true," he said. "I've been seen with a woman or two." His smile widened. "Or three."

"Never all at once, I hope," Charlotte quipped. Then

she chuckled. "I should have specified that it's the marriage-conscious females you avoid."

"Exactly. And can you blame me when nearly fifty percent of all marriages in this country end in divorce?"

Charlotte sighed. "You sound like a hardened divorce attorney."

"I *am* a hardened divorce attorney." Ryan sipped from his coffee cup.

"Well, if you ask me," Charlotte went on, "it's just not healthy...this idea you have of going through life alone."

"I'm not alone," he told her, his voice soft and serious. "I have family. I have friends."

"Which brings us back to your friend, Jim Richards." Charlotte frowned. "And the man's—"

"Marriage-*addicted* daughter, Cherry," Ryan finished for her. He set his cup into its saucer, the mention of the red-haired, man-hunter sending him into a panic once again. "Jim's a good friend, Charlotte. He's been like a father to me ever since my own dad died. It's because of Jim that I took the plunge and moved to Wilmington to open my own office. I don't want to do anything to damage our relationship."

"Well, Cherry's certainly set her sights on you," Charlotte said. "The woman has called this house every day since you arrived in town."

"Yeah...at first I was hoping she was simply calling to offer her support and friendship."

Charlotte actually snorted at his naiveté. "In your wildest dreams, maybe," she said. "It's because of Cherry Richards that the divorce rate has skyrocketed. Didn't she just leave her husband a few months ago?"

"Mm-hmm," Ryan commented. "Her *third* husband."

With a grin, Charlotte remarked, "Looks like she's trying to line you up as number four."

"I'll run naked through Carpenter Park before I let that happen." Ryan ran agitated fingers through his hair. He didn't want to have anything to do with Cherry Richards. The woman might be gorgeous, but she was trouble, no matter how a man spelled it. Yet, hurting Jim's feelings was definitely out of the question as far as Ryan was concerned.

He rubbed the pad of his thumb on the rim of his coffee cup. "And I still haven't figured out what I'm going to do about Friday night. This party Jim is throwing to welcome me to town will be attended by some of the city's most prominent business people."

Another sigh escaped his cousin's lips. "I'd have probably been invited…if I were still married to Harry." She laughed at Ryan's pitying expression. "Don't look at me like that. Divorcing that two-timing idiot was the best thing I ever did. I'm happier than ever. Really."

Ryan smiled.

Charlotte's grin was huge. "I'm just sorry Cherry didn't contract Gold Ribbon to do the catering at this shindig."

"You've got an indomitable spirit," Ryan told her.

She shrugged. "Back to your problem. Friday's party. You think Cherry has ulterior motives about hosting her father's little get-together?"

Ryan planted his elbow on the table. "Of course she does." Then he shook his head. "I'm sorry, Charlotte. I've been dwelling on this all morning…all *week*, actually."

"Don't you dare apologize. I want to help you." Charlotte lifted her chin. "That's why I suggested that you need a woman."

Ryan groaned loudly, nestling his forehead in the palm of his hand. "We're back to that again?"

"Now, hear me out." She swatted at his arm to get him to pay attention. "If you take a date with you—"

"Charlotte!" Ryan's eyes grew large and a spontaneous laugh burst from him. Why hadn't he thought of this days ago? Taking a date along with him to the party would gently and surely convince Cherry Richards that he wasn't interested in a relationship. "You're brilliant!"

His cousin's mouth tipped up at one corner. "Why, thank you."

Ryan laced his fingers and tapped his chin with his knuckle. "Okay," he said. "So...who can I take?"

"Hey, I'm brilliant," Charlotte said, "but I don't have all the answers."

Immediately, Julia Jones entered his thoughts. Actually, she'd flitted in and out of his mind for days. He hadn't seen her since last weekend when he'd barged in on her in this very room. He'd heard Charlotte on the phone with her business partner daily, but he hadn't allowed himself to ask his cousin about Julia. He hadn't wanted to seem too...interested. Because he wasn't, a little voice silently intoned. But now, with the party and all, he was desperate for a woman. Desperate for a date. So inquiring about Julia might not be such a bad idea.

"Some things," Charlotte continued, "a man has to come up with on his own."

A sudden nervousness had him swallowing and moistening his lips. "What about your friend...Julia Jones?"

His cousin's expression evinced a total surprise at his suggestion.

"Well," he said when Charlotte didn't speak, "is the woman available for a date? Is she married?"

"No," Charlotte said after a moment, "she isn't married. So I guess that means she's available to be asked out for Friday night. But..." One eye narrowed and she shook her head.

"What?" Ryan didn't like the negative vibes that suddenly hummed in the air.

"Nothing really," she said. "It's just that in all the months that Julia and I have been partners in Gold Ribbon, she's never once mentioned going out on a date. She's pretty private about that part of her life." Charlotte's face brightened. "But then again, what with my going through those rough months after my divorce, maybe she was just being polite by avoiding the subject of men in general."

Unlacing his fingers, Ryan absently rubbed his temple. His interest was piqued. He could ask Charlotte a dozen questions about Julia right now and was certain his cousin would tell him all she knew. But Ryan didn't. For some reason he felt a sudden intense need to find out about the dark-eyed beauty all on his own. And Friday night's party was just the excuse he needed to do it.

But you're only interested enough to see if the woman is available to save you from Cherry's manicured clutches, the rational part of his conscience was quick to point out.

"Of course," he whispered under his breath.

He slid the now-tepid coffee away from him and stood up. "I'm going to call Julia," he told Charlotte. "As soon as I get to the office. Maybe she'll be willing to help me out." Then he sensibly added, "Just this once."

Chapter Three

Moistening the flap of the final envelope, Julia slid her fingers along the glued edges and placed the publicity advertisement on top of the stack on her desk. The pile wobbled and Julia slapped her hand on it before it could topple over.

"Sheesh," she grumbled, snatching a fat rubber band from the corner of her desk and securing it around the envelopes. "I gotta hire someone to do these mailings."

She made a mental note to visit the post office that afternoon and then turned her attention to the billing. But the numbers quickly blurred as she wondered what Kelly was doing up there in her room.

Silence had been like a live entity that stalked through the house ever since the fight she and Kelly had engaged in this past weekend. Julia could still hardly believe how her daughter had defied the rules. How had Kelly come to the conclusion that such behavior would be tolerated? How could she have thought she could sneak out of the house and not be punished?

Kelly hadn't expected to be caught, a tiny voice intoned silently in Julia's head. That was the crux of the matter.

But what totally baffled Julia was the idea that her fourteen-year-old daughter would even conceive such a rebellious act. It wasn't as though Julia was an ogre of a parent. No, she was nothing like her own father had been. She felt that as a mother, she was open to communication. Open to discussion on any problem Kelly might have.

However, Julia couldn't help but remember how she'd shut down completely when Kelly had brought up the topic of dating. Julia simply hadn't been able to even think about Kelly going out with boys, let alone talk about the subject. So she'd refused to discuss it.

Well, no parent in their right mind would blame her for that! Kelly was only fourteen. Barely a budding teen.

A budding teen with strong opinions, Julia thought. Her daughter's harsh words of criticism flowed over her like vinegar on an open cut. It hurt Julia to know that Kelly thought of her as a workaholic who didn't have a life outside of Gold Ribbon Catering. And Julia was frightened to imagine that Kelly might make good on her immature threat to ignore the rules just because she didn't agree with how Julia chose to live her life.

Kelly was just a child. Too young to be making potentially life-altering decisions that she had it in her mind to make.

So far this week Kelly had adhered to the punishment Julia had doled out. The teen had stayed in the house, turning down every request her friends had made that she go to the movies or to the mall. But when Kelly looked at her, the child's eyes held a deep resentment, and that alarmed Julia. Was there nothing she could do to bridge the gap that yawned wide between the two of them?

She rubbed at her temples, and then picked up the pencil, intent to focus on the numbers in front of her. At least the columns of figures were something in her life over which she could exert some control.

The phone jangled and she jumped, but when it didn't ring a second time, she knew Kelly must have picked up the upstairs extension. The caller was most probably one of her daughter's friends. If someone was calling about a catering job, Julia felt confident that Kelly would speak courteously and quickly pass the call on to her.

She was rechecking the final billing figures when Kelly showed up at her office door. The interest lighting her daughter's dark gaze was unmistakable.

"What is it, Kell?" Julia asked.

"The phone call's for you," she said, her tone saturated with curiosity. "It's a man."

"Okay." Julia reached for the phone as she spoke, but she didn't take her eyes off Kelly's odd expression. "It's probably just someone needing some catering done."

"I don't think so."

Julia's hand froze a scant inch above the telephone receiver. "What do you mean?"

Kelly shrugged. "Just somethin' about his voice."

A frown bit into Julia's brow as her gaze latched onto the phone. Sensing that her daughter was rooted to the spot in the office doorway, she picked up the receiver before she even allowed herself to ponder the caller's identity.

"Julia Jones," she said, using her usual friendly-yet-professional business tone.

"Hi, Julia—"

There was no need for the man to identify himself. Ryan Shane's velvety voice had echoed in her dreams, possessed her night fantasies, to the point of frustration.

"It's Ryan Shane."

"Yes," she said, feeling an odd reluctance to greet him by name. Terribly aware of Kelly's presence, Julia felt a slow heat rise to her face. "H-how are you?" she stammered awkwardly.

Her heartbeat seemed to go berserk in her chest, her hands trembled. What the hell was the matter with her?

"Oh," he said, chuckling lightly, "I'm fine, I guess. But I won't lie to you...I could be better."

Was that nervousness she detected in his voice? she wondered. She couldn't say for certain because she was too preoccupied with her body's unanticipated reaction to the low rumble of his laughter. The sound was sexy. No. *Provocative* described it much better.

A shiver skittered up her spine and she had to work hard to repress an actual physical tremble. She'd rather wither away and die than have Kelly see what the sound of this man's voice was doing to her. She wished the child would go away, give her a little privacy, but Julia couldn't bring herself to look toward her daughter, let alone shoo her from the doorway. Darn it, Julia condemned herself silently, what was happening here?

The implication of his last statement hit her. "Well, ah, Ryan—"

The instant she said his name, Julia detected movement from the corner of her eye. Kelly came to stand at the corner of her desk.

"Is something wrong?" she finished. Then her nervousness had her rephrasing the question before he had a chance to speak. "Is there something I can do for you?"

"There sure is," Ryan said.

The acute awkwardness Kelly's presence caused finally got the best of Julia and she tossed her daughter a blatantly dismissing look hoping she would get the silent message regarding her need for some privacy. However, Kelly seemed oblivious to the plea Julia knew was expressed in her eyes. The intense curiosity radiating from the child glowed with an unmistakable incandescence that had Kelly leaning forward.

"How about going out with me tomorrow night?"

Julia had lifted her hand to signal Kelly to leave the room, but Ryan's soft-spoken question wiped all thought from her brain. Her arm fell, limp, to her side.

"I beg your pardon?" she said.

"I've been invited to a party tomorrow night," Ryan told her. "And I'd like for you to go with me."

"Oh, I couldn't do that." The words passed her lips automatically.

"Couldn't do what?" Kelly asked.

Her daughter's frantic whisper was like an annoying honey bee buzzing near her ear.

"Aw, come on, Julia…"

His tone even silkier than it had been when he'd asked her out and Julia felt renewed heat flush her face.

"I really haven't been in town long enough to get to know anyone," he said.

A sudden thought had Julia asking, "Did Charlotte put you up to this?"

"Put *who* up to *what?*" Kelly whispered.

Julia glared her daughter into silence.

"Actually," Ryan said, "Charlotte seemed to think my asking you out wasn't a very good idea."

"She's right. It isn't a good idea."

"What isn't a good idea?" This time Kelly's question was louder.

"Ryan," Julia asked, "would you hold on just a minute?" She pressed the telephone receiver against her chest so her next words wouldn't be overheard. Her lips pursed together as she stared at her daughter. "Would you mind taking your nosy self out of my office?"

"Who is it, Mom?"

"Go," was all Julia said, and she pointed toward the door with her free hand.

Kelly grumbled, but turned and took a couple of reluctant steps toward the door.

Pressing the phone to her ear, she said, "I'm sorry, Ryan. I'm here."

"I really do need a date for this party," Ryan pleaded softly. "It's a business dinner. A one-time thing. I could really use your help."

The deep timbre of his voice caressed her skin like a summer breeze, heated and enticing. Experiencing its seductive fluidness on top of the prickly irritation she'd felt at Kelly's snooping had Julia feeling sure her senses were going haywire.

"I'm sorry, Ryan," she said again. "But I just don't..." Why was she finding it so hard to come up with the words she needed to politely turn down his offer? "*Do* that sort of thing."

Again, Ryan's rich, almost murmuring, chuckle came over the line, and Julia helplessly closed her eyes to let the full effect of the sensual sound course through her.

"What don't you do?" he asked. "Go out on dates? Or help people out?"

She actually smiled at his teasing. But the implication of his questions had a deep impact on her. If he only knew the truth—

"You don't do *what* sort of thing?"

Julia's gaze swung toward the door where Kelly had poked her head from around the corner.

Again, Julia clamped her hand over the receiver. "Kelly Marie!"

"Mom, if that guy is asking you out on a date," her daughter rushed to whisper at her, "then you should most definitely go. I heard you mention Charlotte...that she had put him up to this. If this guy's a friend of Charlotte's, he must be okay. I mean, just think of it. A date! You'd have fun for once in your life."

There was no maliciousness in Kelly's hushed and hurried tone. In fact, what Julia saw in her daughter's dark eyes was a light of caring. Kelly was excited at the prospect of her mother having a fun evening. Julia hadn't witnessed this kind of tender and emotional outpouring from Kelly in a long time.

If Julia were to go out with Ryan, it would show Kelly that she was making an effort to compromise on their differences. Maybe then Kelly would be more willing to compromise, too. More willing to follow the rules.

But how could she accept Ryan's offer when she'd already as good as turned him down?

"Julia?"

She loved the way her name rolled off his tongue, soft and sexy.

"I'm here," she told him. "I'm just...thinking."

Guilt crept up on her. She didn't like the idea of having ulterior motives behind going out on a date with Ryan. It wasn't fair to him.

Glancing up at Kelly, she saw her daughter's open, encouraging smile. And her mind was made up.

"W-well, Ryan," she said, hating the clumsy quality

of her voice. "If it will help you out, then I'd be happy to go."

"Great!"

Kelly's gleeful squeal nearly drowned out Ryan's response. Julia motioned for her daughter to be quiet while she got more particulars from Ryan as to the time he'd pick her up tomorrow night. Finally she placed the receiver back into the cradle.

She gazed up at her daughter and shrugged. "Looks like I'm going on a date."

"Oh, Mom," Kelly said, giving her a quick hug, "I can't wait. Can I call Sheila?"

Julia nearly chuckled at the sight of her daughter prancing from one foot to the other.

"Go ahead," she said, and had to smile when Kelly rushed out of the room, obviously intending to use the phone upstairs to make her call.

All alone in her office, Julia glanced down at the phone and groaned. "What have I done?" She rested her chin on her palm, her elbow on the arm of her desk chair.

She'd have to tell Ryan—right up front—that she wasn't interested in any kind of relationship. She didn't have to be so honest as to tell him she was only going out on the date to make an impression on Kelly. However, it wouldn't be fair of her to lead him on in any way. She'd have to set him straight right away.

But a tiny jolt of anticipation sizzled along her nerve endings at the thought of actually going out with Ryan.

"Don't get yourself too excited," she murmured to herself. "Because there will only be this one date." Heaving a sigh tinged with something that sounded suspiciously like regret, she softly but firmly repeated, "Just one."

* * *

Julia pressed her palm to her jittery stomach, stared at her reflection in the full-length mirror and groaned. "I can't believe I'm doing this."

The lamentation had passed her lips at least a hundred times since she'd agreed to go out with Ryan.

"Mom, you look great." Kelly sat on the bed behind Julia, barely containing her excitement as she gazed into the same mirror at her mother.

"This dress is too short," Julia lamented.

Kelly rolled her eyes. "It's two inches above your knee. If anything, it's not short enough."

Tossing a narrow-eyed look over her shoulder, Julia plunked her fist on her hip. "I'd expect you to say that."

Kelly got up from where she sat and physically moved her mother's hand back down to her side. "You'll wrinkle the silk."

The simple cut and squared-off neckline of the dress was classy and elegant, and the whisper-soft material felt exquisite against her skin. She and Kelly had spent several hours in various department stores picking out the deep purple cocktail dress and the accessories to go with it. And those hours had created a new and special bond between them.

The concern in Kelly's warning squeezed at Julia's heart.

A soft sigh passed Julia's lips as she caught her daughter's eye in the mirror. She reached out and hooked her pinkie finger with Kelly's. "I wouldn't have been able to do this without you, you know."

Kelly grinned. "You do look great."

"You don't think these earrings are too much?"

"No way," she said. "They're all glittery and beautiful. They match you perfectly."

Julia smiled. "Thanks."

"Are you nervous?" Kelly asked.

She shrugged. "A little." It was a bold-faced lie. She was so nervous she felt about ready to throw up.

When the front doorbell rang, mother and daughter turned to face one another.

"He's here." Kelly's tone could almost be described as a squeal.

Julia couldn't stop the low moan that escaped her throat. "I can't believe I'm doing this."

Ignoring her mother's complaint, Kelly moved toward the bedroom door. "I'll go let him in. You wait a minute or so and then make an awesome entrance."

Her daughter's suggestion seemed sophomoric at best. But Kelly had already disappeared around the corner, her footsteps scampering hastily down the steps.

Why was she so trembly inside? Julia wondered. Maybe it was because she was going out with Ryan Shane under false pretenses. This date had nothing whatsoever to do with Ryan. Julia was going out with this man to prove a point to her daughter, guilt about that fact be damned.

She took a last look at her reflection. Running her fingers through her short, wavy tousle of hair, she couldn't stop the slow grin from spreading on her mouth. It sure didn't hurt the situation that Ryan Shane was so…easy on the eyes. Her smile widened wickedly.

"Now, stop that," she chastised herself. That kind of thinking would only get her into trouble.

However, she was still smiling as she grabbed her brand new evening bag off the bed and went out the door.

Midway down the staircase, she stopped when both

Kelly and Ryan turned to face her. Her breath tripped in her throat. Lord, she'd forgotten how blue his eyes were.

The appreciation glittering in Ryan's gaze had her whole body humming with nervous energy. Her heart hammered so loudly she was sure he'd be able to hear.

His smoke-gray suit set off his tawny hair to perfection, the double-breasted jacket accentuating his broad shoulders and flat stomach. The image of his taut, naked abs flashed through her mind and Julia had to forcefully shove the thought aside. Steeling herself with a deep inhalation, she smiled and descended the few remaining steps.

"Hi, Ryan," she greeted. "I see you've met my daughter. Kelly, this is Ryan Shane, Charlotte's cousin."

The introduction came out so stiff, so awkward, Julia feared she'd set the tone for the evening. But Ryan smiled that boyish grin of his, and it looked as if Kelly just might melt in her shoes right there where she stood. The two of them exchanged pleasantries, and Julia indulged in a moment of maternal pride as she watched her daughter converse with Ryan.

The sudden heat she felt flushing her skin alerted her that Ryan's attention was once again focused on her. Raising her gaze to his, she felt her heart clunk against her ribs. The man was handsome enough to steal away a woman's breath.

"You look great," he said.

Kelly reached out and touched her arm. "See, Mom. I told you."

"Thanks," Julia breathed, surprised that it seemed to take all her strength to say the tiny word.

The three of them stood there in a fleeting moment of silence before Ryan commented, "We should probably go."

"Of course," Julia said. And then she turned to Kelly. "I won't be too late." She hesitated, but couldn't keep herself from asking, "You'll be all right...here?"

She knew Kelly was old enough to take care of herself. That really wasn't what she was asking. The mother in Julia wanted to know that Kelly would stay home, where she was supposed to be.

Kelly got the message, loud and clear. After only the smallest rolling of her eyes, she said, "I'll be right here." Then her gaze softened. "And I'll be fine."

Julia reached out and squeezed her daughter's fingers. The silent message was meant to convey the appreciation she felt of having her fears alleviated. Kelly smiled and returned the pressure, and there was no mistaking the good-luck wish gleaming in her daughter's eyes.

With love swelling her heart, Julia hoped this new bond she'd formed with Kelly remained strong.

She turned to face Ryan. "I'm ready."

But as she walked through the door into the evening, she wondered just how ready she could be. She hadn't been out on a date in so long. It wasn't as if she'd never been in contact with men. Working with the public as a caterer, she'd met plenty of them. And one or two had even expressed an interest in her. But she hadn't allowed herself more than a date or two with any one man. A close relationship was something she simply couldn't afford. For her own well-being. For her own protection.

As Ryan held the car door open for her, she smiled at him and realized that this date was different. She was going into it knowing there wouldn't be another. She didn't have to worry about a relationship developing. Ryan had said it himself. He'd described this date as a one-time thing.

Leaning against the seat back, Julia felt all the tension leave her. She could relax and have a good time.

Ryan slid behind the steering wheel and started the engine. "Kelly's beautiful," he said.

"Thanks." Julia felt a rush of pride and pleasure surge through her at Ryan's compliment.

He glanced at her. "She looks just like you."

Julia was happy that he immediately put the car into gear and pulled into traffic. She wouldn't want him to see how he'd affected her. She'd forgotten how nice it was to be flattered by a man.

"By the way," she said. "Did I tell you how distinguished you look? Like a cool and competent businessman."

He grinned his thanks. "That's exactly what I need." After a moment he said, "I don't mind telling you that I'm feeling nervous about tonight. Meeting Wilmington's professional elite can be a little daunting."

"You'll be great," Julia told him. "Don't worry."

Their friendly banter continued on the short drive across town. Ryan pulled into the driveway flanking the large stone house and parked.

"Well," he said, "here we are."

Julia got out of the car, absently smoothing her hand down the gossamer fabric of her dress. She was too preoccupied with Ryan's growing anxiety to think much about how she looked. When they reached the door and Ryan pressed the buzzer, she slipped her hand in his, intending to lend him some strength and calm his distress. Her reward for the action was seeing his azure gaze light with a deep and serious appreciation. A shiver coursed along her spine, but before she could savor the moment, the door opened and Julia was faced with the most beautiful woman she'd ever met.

"Ryan!" the woman greeted warmly. "Come in."

Ryan obeyed her command, fairly dragging Julia through the door with him. When the woman stepped up to kiss him full on the mouth, Julia tried to release Ryan's hand. It seemed the polite thing to do, yet Ryan held tight. Sheesh, Julia thought, he really is nervous about meeting these people.

"Cherry," Ryan said at last, "I'd like you to meet Julia Jones. Julia, this is Cherry Richards. She and her father Jim have been kind enough to throw this party for me."

Ryan was forced to let go of Julia's hand so she could properly greet Cherry Richards. Julia mouthed all the right words, all the while marveling at the woman's tumble of red hair and her sexy sea-green eyes.

"Do you mind if I ask how you and Ryan met?" Cherry chuckled to cover the rudeness of her blatant question. "I mean, he's only been in town a week. And what with searching for office space and an apartment, I'm surprised he's found the time to meet someone so…pretty."

Julia barely suppressed a grin at the backhanded compliment, and she decided suddenly that this beautiful woman was reeking with jealousy. Jealousy of *her*. Julia wanted to laugh out loud, knowing that next to this woman she looked like a plain Jane.

Meaning to put Cherry's mind at ease, Julia said, "You're very beautiful, yourself. That dress is lovely on you."

Cherry's plastic smile confused her, and she decided to change the subject. "Actually, Ryan and I met through Charlotte, Ryan's cousin. In fact, Charlotte is my business partner."

"Oh, yes," Cherry said. "I'd heard that Charlotte had

to go to work after her divorce. Poor woman. She's a cook or something…''

The woman's catty tone made Julia's jaw tighten. ''Our company is called Gold Ribbon Catering. Maybe you've heard of us. Charlotte's our chef.'' Then she added, ''She's an excellent chef.''

Just then Ryan curled his fingers around Julia's upper arm. ''Julia and I might have just met, Cherry,'' he said suddenly. ''But we've become—'' he gazed at Julia ''—very close.''

His odd remark had Julia glancing his way. Since the conversation had been focused at that moment on Charlotte and Gold Ribbon, Ryan's comment seemed to fall out of the blue. It landed like a stone.

Julia looked at the tiny beads of perspiration dotting his brow. The insult she felt on Charlotte's behalf due to Cherry's rude remarks was forgotten as she worried about the man at her side. Ryan was so nervous about meeting the people at this party. She slid her palm over his fingers and smiled into his face, hoping she could assuage his dread.

''Shall we?'' Cherry said, leading them into the house. ''I was serving cocktails out on the deck.''

The pressure of Ryan's hand at the small of Julia's back was endearing…almost intimate, and she found herself smiling into his face.

She was happy to discover that she knew several of the people present. Not that she traveled in the same circles as these lawyers, doctors and company CEOs, but she'd been hired by some of them. She'd catered a birthday party for one, an anniversary party for another, and a fairly large company picnic for a third. And the nice thing about it was that they greeted her as if she were an old friend, which made it easy for her to introduce

Ryan. Soon, he was relaxed and talking, and Julia was relieved to see his fit of nerves had subsided.

When Ryan introduced her to Cherry's father Jim, Julia could see that Ryan held the man in high esteem. The elderly man clapped the younger one on the shoulder and a deep affection and friendship emanated from the two men.

At one point before dinner Julia was involved in a lively conversation with another couple when Ryan suddenly appeared at her side. He smoothly joined the discussion, but Julia noticed something about him the others in the small circle didn't. Ryan's gaze inadvertantly darted across the room several times. Julia glanced up to see Cherry standing at the bar watching him closely. When the redhead saw that Julia had noticed, she busied herself rearranging glasses.

The roasted chicken served at dinner was moist and tender, even if the main dish was ho-hum in her estimation. The vegetables were coated in a ginger sauce that was quite delicious, and she would have enjoyed them thoroughly if Ryan hadn't begun talking like a parrot on speed. Cherry, seated to his left, hung on his every word.

It was so strange that Ryan seemed nervous one minute and poised and professional the next. The fluctuation in Ryan's emotional state was getting to Julia and she reached under the table to pat his knee in comfort, but that only seemed to upset him more. Another full hour passed before Julia finally caught on to what, exactly, was happening.

Like a good hostess, Cherry had planned well by serving a buffet-style dessert in the large game room, a strategy obviously meant to force the guests to mingle. During this time Ryan stuck to Julia's side as though the two of them had been bolted at the hip. And that's when she realized that it wasn't the guests who were making Ryan nervous—it was Cherry.

Every time the radiant redhead came within three feet of him, his words would accelerate, his blue eyes would become almost panic-stricken. Oh, he hid it well, Julia thought. She was certain the other party guests didn't perceive the change in him. But she did, and whenever his behavior altered, Julia would look up and, sure enough, Cherry was in close proximity.

Cherry Richards wanted Ryan. *And he knew it!*

He hadn't wanted a date for this evening. He'd wanted a sentinel. Someone who could protect him from the luscious and lovely Cherry Richards. It was laughable, really. A hilarious situation.

Why, then, Julia wondered, did the idea tick her off? Why did it make her feel so...used?

Those feelings only seemed to grow through the remainder of the evening, and by the time the thank-yous and farewells were said, Julia's emotions had turned dark and brooding.

It's only one date, she reminded herself. After tonight you never have to see Ryan again. With that thought planted firmly in her mind, Julia almost made it home without telling him how she was feeling. Almost, but not quite.

When Ryan parked on her street several doors down from her brownstone, he turned that darned boyish smile on her and said, "Thanks, Julia."

It was just too much, and the anger in her exploded.

"Never, in my whole life—" her teeth were clenched tightly together "—have I felt so used!"

Chapter Four

The wide-eyed surprise expressed on Ryan's handsome face would have been comical...at any other time, any other place. But the fury burning in Julia was white-hot.

"You're angry?"

"Anger doesn't *begin* to describe what I'm feeling."

She stared out the window into the night. "'I'm surprised Ryan's had time to meet someone so...pretty,'" Julia mimicked Cherry's comment, putting extraordinarily ugly emphasis on the final word. Clutching her purse in her lap, she barely repressed her urge to scream in frustration. "I couldn't understand how someone so beautiful could be jealous of my looks. I actually tried to make her feel better by complimenting her appearance. Her dress." She exhaled forcefully. "I feel so stupid."

She faced Ryan. "That woman wasn't jealous of my looks. She was jealous of me—*being with you.* Cherry Richards wants you." The short statement was nothing less than an accusation. "And you know it. You knew it all along. You didn't take me to that party because you wanted a date. You took me because you needed a guard dog."

A groan escaped her as she thought of how cozily, how intimately, Ryan had touched her during the party. But only within eyeshot of Cherry.

"You told that woman we're *very close*," she accused. "What a joke. What a lie."

"Now, Julia..."

The silky sound of his voice made her madder than ever. She needed to get out of this car. Away from him.

Why the hell was she so angry? The question pestered her as she shoved open the door. She had no answer. All she knew was that her head was filled to the brim with red-hot fury.

She was cognizant of Ryan exiting the car as she fumbled frantically with the seat belt latch. Finally, it gave. Pushing her way out of the seat, she heard a tiny ripping sound.

"My dress," she breathed, standing by the car. "My brand new dress."

The light cast by the street lamp splintered into narrow shards as tears blurred her vision. She was a wreck! A mess. All she wanted to do was get inside her house where she'd be safe from this humiliating experience.

"Julia, stop." Ryan grasped her upper arms with both his hands. "I'm sorry. I'll have your dress repaired. Better yet, I'll buy you a new one."

"I don't want a new dress," she said, trying to shrug him off. But he held firm. "I want this one. And I want it just the way it was."

Her request was infantile, she knew. She was acting like a big baby. But she was so upset she couldn't have stopped the whine from tumbling from her lips even if she'd tried.

"Let go, Ryan. I want to go inside."

"Listen to me for just a minute." Then he softly added, "Please, Julia."

She dashed a tear from her cheek and stopped struggling, but she couldn't lift her gaze to his.

"Everything you've said is true. Cherry Richards wants me."

Julia sensed rather than saw him grimace.

"That sounds so damned conceited," he said. "But it's true. And I did take you along as a kind of...shield. You see, I'm not interested in getting involved with Cherry. I'm not interested in getting involved with *any* woman."

The last comment insulted her, and for the life of her she couldn't figure out why. Then suddenly her ire was stirred up all over again.

"Well then," she said, glaring at him, "we're like peas in a pod. Because I'm not interested in getting involved with any man."

One hand slid down to cup her elbow. "Look, Julia, I needed your help. I did tell you that right up front. But I certainly didn't mean to hurt you."

Julia blinked and took a deep breath. Finally she asked, "Why can't you tell Cherry? You know, that you're not interested?" One corner of her mouth quirked up with humorless irony. "You certainly didn't have a problem telling me."

Ryan stared off into the night. Then he looked her in the eyes. "It's a difficult situation. Jim is like a father to me. He's helped me so much over the years. And he's promised to help me again. In getting my new practice off the ground."

He dropped his hand from her elbow, but his other hand still clasped her arm. "But Cherry is his daughter. And blood really is thicker than water. She could ruin my relationship with Jim. And she's the kind of woman who would do it. If she didn't get her way."

Julia hated to admit it, but she understood. She cocked her head a fraction. "Why didn't you tell me? Why didn't you let me in on what was going on?"

The tiny exhalation that burst from Ryan was full of disdain.

"And what was I supposed to say?" he asked derisively. "'Julia, would you let me hide behind your skirt'?"

"Well, that's exactly what you wanted," she said pointedly, and immediately felt mean. "I'm sorry. I shouldn't have said that."

"You have no cause to apologize. You only stated the truth." He sighed. "The situation made me feel so foolish. But I felt backed into a corner." His gaze was miserable as he added, "And I just didn't know what else to do."

The unadulterated wretchedness in his blue eyes touched her, and her first impulse was to reach out to him. To console him when he seemed most vulnerable.

She certainly didn't have to worry that he'd misconstrue any solace she might offer. He'd made it clear he wasn't interested in her as a woman. And he'd rectified his wrong, hadn't he? He'd fessed up to the crazy scheme he'd involved her in. So there really wasn't any reason she shouldn't try to soothe away the guilt and self-degradation he was feeling. In fact, it seemed she had every reason *to* reach out to him.

But she simply couldn't bring herself to do it. There

was still some unnameable prickle of irritation she felt because of what he'd done. And worse, what he'd said.

"Boy," she finally said, "we certainly have bungled this date, haven't we?"

He chuckled and Julia could clearly see it wasn't an easy task for him.

"I take full responsibility," Ryan said.

After only a moment of hesitation, Julia said, "I agree."

His face took on that wide-eyed surprise for the second time that evening, and Julia couldn't help but laugh. Ryan quickly joined her.

"Oh," she finally said, "all in all, I guess I did have a good time tonight. Thanks for the evening." She reached her hand out toward him.

"No way," he told her. "I'm walking you to your door."

"You don't have to do that."

"Of course I do. We're nearly half a block from your house and it's close to eleven at night. What would my mother say if—"

"Okay, okay," she said with a grin. "I certainly don't want to be the cause of your mother giving you any grief."

They walked along the sidewalk, and even though they weren't touching, Julia was very aware of his presence beside her. The summer night felt sultry after the car's air-conditioned interior, and Ryan's woodsy cologne hung heavy in the air. They went up the steps and stood at the door.

"Well, here we are," Julia said. Then she smiled. "Your mom would be proud."

Behind Ryan, the sheer curtains of the living room

window stirred and Julia felt a sudden wave of panic wash over her.

Ryan opened his mouth to speak, but her quick approach toward him cut off whatever he was about to say.

"I know this is very awkward," Julia whispered frantically. "But would you mind kissing me good-night?" When a frown was his only response, she added, "I'll explain everything. I promise. Just kiss me. Quick."

She tasted of fire and spice. So sizzling and spirited that Ryan felt as though he'd just bitten into a jalapeño pepper. And the sensation took him totally by surprise. The urge to pull away from her hot, moist mouth and take a mind-cooling breath was strong, but he resisted. He'd been fantasizing about kissing this woman for a full week...ever since he'd met her. Hey, he might not be willing to admit such a thing to anyone else, but he could certainly be honest with himself.

He caressed her soft, silky lips with his, marveling that the reality of this kiss was the exact opposite of what he'd imagined. He'd thought she'd taste of heated sunshine, or soft summer rain. But this heady zest was like a swift kick in the chest. If a man wasn't careful, he'd be knocked to his knees in the blink of an eye.

Wrapping his arms around her trim body, he let his hand trail up her back. His blood was just beginning to pound through him when...

It was over.

She reached up on her tiptoes, hooked her chin over his shoulder and hugged him to her. The feel of her breasts pressed up tightly against his chest was almost as good as the kiss they'd shared, and Ryan returned the hug.

Julia Jones was a complicated woman. She could be

friendly and vivacious in a crowd of strangers...Ryan had watched her make a roomful of friends tonight. She could be gentle and caring. He'd been on the receiving end of her tender doting when she kept reassuring him he'd do just fine at the party. But Julia could also be very blunt and honest about her feelings if she was distressed or angry. He'd certainly witnessed that, too. However, it was Julia's sultry side he was liking more and more.

"Perfect," she whispered in his ear. "Just perfect."

Well...if she thought that tiny, little meeting of their lips could be described as a perfect kiss, he had news for her. He could do better than that.

"Here," he murmured huskily, pulling back from her and gently tipping up her chin with his fingers, "let me show you what perfect really is."

Her stunned expression alone would have stopped his slow forward momentum, but the flat of her hand slapping against his chest was like a douse of cold water on glowing embers. Confusion wrinkled his brow and he straightened.

"That's not necessary," she said. "She's gone."

Now he was totally bewildered. "Who's gone?" he asked, shaking his head the tiniest fraction.

"Kelly."

Her tone gave him the impression that she expected that one name to explain everything. It didn't. And he was sure the quandary he experienced was clearly expressed in his gaze.

Finally, Julia seemed to catch on. "Well, Kelly was at the window. I wanted to make certain I looked as if I'd had a wonderful evening. That I was enjoying all the...extras a fourteen-year-old would expect when two adults go out on a date. I needed Kelly to see that I was having a…good time." Then she added, "That's why I went out with you."

Her onyx eyes raised to his, mortification exposed for him to see. Obviously she'd let something slip. What it was, he still wasn't certain. But he meant to find out.

"I get the impression," he said, a good-natured smile playing at one corner of his mouth, "that I wasn't the only one who ventured on this date with ulterior motives."

Julia tried to look away, but he captured her jaw in his palm and guided her gaze back to his.

"Julia?"

She moistened those luscious lips of hers and he felt a pang of regret to realize her "perfect" description unfortunately hadn't been a recounting of their kiss, as he'd first imagined.

"Well," she began slowly, "you see…I've been having a little trouble with my daughter." As if stalling for time, she clarified, "Kelly."

"Yes, I've met Kelly." Ryan could clearly see that Julia was experiencing an awkwardness at having to admit whatever it was she was about to admit. And he loved her discomfort! She'd made him feel horribly guilty about having used her as a shield of protection against Cherry. Well, now it was Julia's turn to squirm. "But what does she have to do with our date?"

A small, nervous laugh escaped from Julia's long and slender throat. "You're just going to laugh when you hear this."

After a quiet moment Ryan said, "I'm sure I will. If I ever do get to hear it."

Julia sighed, then shifted her weight. "Look, Ryan," she said, her tone suddenly serious. "Dating is not an activity I normally…participate in. It's nothing against you…or any other man. It's just that I feel a tremendous need to protect myself.''

He watched her press her lips together, as if she felt she'd revealed more than she'd meant to.

''Anyway,'' she continued, ''my daughter has recently shown signs of rebellion. We've fought. She doesn't want to follow the rules I've set down for her.''

Ryan could tell this subject was upsetting to Julia. In the hope of making this easier for her, he shrugged, smiled and commented, ''What kid does?''

Appreciation illuminated her dark gaze. ''Yeah, well, it seems that Kelly feels I work too much. That I don't have enough…fun. And she doesn't want me making rules for her when…''

The sentence trailed, and Julia tucked her bottom lip between her teeth. After heaving a sigh, she explained, ''I went out with you as a way of showing my daughter I'm not a stick-in-the-mud.'' She narrowed her eyes. ''Do you understand?''

He gazed at her for a long, silent moment. Then he reached out and took hold of her hand, her skin feeling smooth and satiny against his. ''We are a pair, you and I,'' he said. ''Me using you. You using me.''

''I really am sorry, Ryan.''

Giving her fingers a gentle squeeze, he said, ''Don't be. I needed you. And you were there for me.''

Her sudden smile was illuminating in the darkness, and Ryan felt his heart kick against his ribs.

''And I'd do it all over again.'' After a quick hesitation, she added, ''Because I would need to…of course.'' She tilted her head toward the house, indicating her problem with Kelly.

Julia and Ryan shared a soft and intimate chuckle before saying their good-nights.

"Hey," he called from the bottom of the porch steps. She was inside the house now, the screen in the door shadowing her face. "Thanks for your help tonight."

She nodded and softly said, "And thank you, too. You can't imagine how this date with you has patched up my relationship with Kelly."

Tossing her a quick smile, he said, "I'm glad."

As Ryan walked away, the strangest feeling crept over him. Like he'd left a piece of himself behind. It was ridiculous, really. But he couldn't shake the feeling that a hunk of his heart had suddenly gone missing.

"Okay..." Charlotte touched Julia on the shoulder to get her attention. "What's the problem?"

Julia blinked her way out of the worried stupor that had her in its clutches. "What are you talking about? I don't have a problem," she lied.

"Sure you don't," Charlotte remarked. "You're just pummeling that bread dough for the heck of it, right?"

Glancing down, Julia saw that she'd kneaded the dough into a creamy-colored mound of elastic silk. Flour dusted her skin up to the elbows, and Julia admitted to herself that she'd gotten lost in the task. She felt guilty, knowing that there was lots to be done for the party Gold Ribbon was catering tonight.

"These rolls will be delicious." Her tone held a lightness she certainly didn't feel inside, and using the back of one wrist, she rubbed at an itch on her chin.

"You're fighting with Kelly again."

Charlotte's knowing statement made Julia groan. "That child is going to give me gray hair."

A grin played across her friend's mouth. "That's exactly why teenagers were invented. Didn't you know that?"

Without thought, Julia began tearing off small pieces of dough and rolling them into balls. "I'm finding it out real quick."

Charlotte peeked into the oven. The rich, heady aroma of roasting beef wafted through the kitchen as she said, "I thought things were great between you two, ever since your date with Ryan."

"Yeah, well..." Julia plunked a ball of dough onto the baking sheet. "That sure didn't last long." Then to herself, she muttered, Not even a full week.

Ripping off another piece of bread dough, she said to Charlotte, "The first couple of days after the date were wonderful. Kelly mooned around with huge calf eyes, asking me details about my date. Then as the week wore on, she began asking why Ryan wasn't calling me...and when we were going out again...and what had I done to mess things up with him. I panicked. I told her flat-out that I hadn't planned on going out with him again." Another small ball of dough was plunked onto the sheet.

She looked over to where Charlotte stood peeling carrots at the sink. "Do you believe that Kelly actually got angry? I told her I was only trying to do what she wanted. She said that one date does not change a person's life-style. And she accused me of going out with Ryan just to mollify *her*."

Charlotte's hands stilled. "But isn't that exactly why you went out with him?"

"Of course," Julia said, her tone blunt. "But Kelly's not supposed to realize that." She could clearly see the laughter fighting to erupt from Charlotte, but her friend was battling it. "Now our relationship is worse than ever. And I just don't know what I'm going to do."

Drying her hands on a tea towel, Charlotte said, "Maybe Ryan would be willing to—"

"No." Julia cut her suggestion to the quick. "No way. He doesn't want to become involved in my problem."

Julia didn't dare admit to Charlotte that spending time with Ryan was the last thing she needed. Her fantasies of the man had been so vivid even before their date. And the past week since they'd gone out, Ryan had haunted her dreams like a sensual wraith. She'd relived their good-night kiss dozens of times in her dreams. In her dreams, however, their kiss was anything but chaste, and Ryan didn't stop his sexual ministrations with his lips...he used his hands, and the rest of his body, as well.

Blinking once slowly to clear him from her mind, Julia focused on rolling the last bit of dough between her palms. No, she needed to stay away from Ryan. Far away. For her own protection. That was why she was careful when coming to Charlotte's house, always calling first to discretely discover that Ryan was at his office.

"Look," Charlotte said, "let's stop and grab a bite of lunch. We can talk about this—"

Just then Ryan rushed through the back door. Julia's eyes widened at the anxious look on his face, and although she hated to admit it, her heart skipped a happy beat at the sight of him.

"Ryan, what is it?" Charlotte asked. "What's wrong?"

His blue eyes were filled with panic. "Thank God I found you! I've been calling you all morning."

The fact that he'd approached her and not Charlotte took Julia completely by surprise. "I w-was out," she stammered. "Shopping for food for the party Charlotte and I are catering tonight."

"You have to come with me," he said. "You have to come with me now."

Without taking her eyes from Ryan's face, Julia groped for the terry towel she'd left on the countertop. She gripped it between her hands, sure that he meant to whisk her away this instant.

"Go where, Ryan?" she asked, hoping to calm him. "And why?" Her eyes narrowed as a thought struck her. "Does this have something to do with Cherry Richards?"

"This has everything to do with Cherry." He looked from Julia to Charlotte and back to Julia.

"Would you take a deep breath," Charlotte told him, "and tell us what's happened?"

"Jim called me this morning," he said. "He told me that Cherry's been working hard all week to find me an apartment. He seemed so proud that his little girl would want to help me out. Apparently, Cherry's found a couple of apartments she thinks would be appropriate and she wants me to go see them with her. This afternoon."

A resurgence of panic crept into his gaze. "You gotta come with me, Julia. We've got to convince Cherry we're a couple."

"But—" Julia shook her head "—why would she do something so bold? Especially after you made it clear that you were...taken?" She felt heat rush to her face, but he didn't seem to notice.

He dragged agitated fingers through his tawny hair. "Cherry stopped by my office twice this week. Unannounced. Uninvited." He sighed. "Although she didn't come right out and say it, I'm sure she thinks our date was a ruse."

Wiping her fingers on the towel, Julia murmured, "She isn't the only one."

Ryan's gaze narrowed. "What do you mean?"

Again, Julia shook her head. "It's nothing." Then she took a deep breath and readied herself to deliver the bad news. "Look, I can't go anywhere with you right now. Charlotte and I have a meal to cook. We have a party to cater—"

"Now, Julia," Charlotte said. "There's really no reason why you couldn't take a couple of hours to go with Ryan. We have to wait for the roasts to finish cooking. And we can't bake the rolls until they've had a chance to rise." She looked up at the clock. "If you're back here by three, we'll have plenty of time to braise the veggies and slice the beef. And then off we go to deliver the meal."

The idea of spending the afternoon with Ryan sent mixed emotions racing through Julia. Elation and dread. Giddiness and apprehension.

"I shouldn't leave everything to you," she said, intending to be firm, but hating the fact that there was very little argument in her voice.

"Besides," Charlotte went on, "won't it be great when you go home tonight and tell Kelly that you spent the afternoon with Ryan?"

Julia stood there for a moment as the suggestion sunk in. "That *would* be great," she helplessly breathed. She would love to get her relationship with Kelly smoothed out again. She longed to once again feel that close mother-daughter bond they had shared just last week.

The towel in her hands drew her attention down the length of her body. "But I'm a mess," she cried. "I can't meet Cherry dressed like this."

"You look great," Ryan said, moving closer. "You look perfect."

He was within arm's reach now, and Julia marveled

at the way the air in the kitchen seemed to compress and become unbreathable. Her heart *ka-chunked* in her chest, a small shiver skittered up her spine. Ryan took the towel from her fingers, and when his skin contacted hers, she felt a tiny jolt of current.

"All except," he whispered, "for this flour on your chin."

As he brushed the soft terry against her skin, Julia's blood rushed through her veins at such a speed she was certain she'd grow light-headed and faint dead away. She had to say something, do something, to break this silly reaction she was having to this man.

"I'm only going so that I can tell Kelly I went."

The statement sounded stiff and forced, even to her ears. But Ryan didn't seem in the least bothered by it.

"Of course," he said smoothly. "And I've only asked you to go so I can get Cherry off my back and save my friendship with Jim." He smiled at her. "Deal?"

She stared at the strong, tanned hand he reached out to her, her pulse pounding in her ears. This would solve all their problems, wouldn't it? If she and Ryan played at being a couple, then Kelly would relax about her mother's workaholic life-style, and Ryan would be safe from the infamous, husband-hunting Cherry.

Why then was she hesitating? As she slid her palm smoothly against his, the answer to her silent question came to her, loud and clear.

Because she was scared. Scared witless.

Chapter Five

As Ryan's car sped toward the city, Julia tried to get a grip on her wayward nerves. The two of them play-acting as a couple really was the perfect solution to all their problems. However, Julia knew deep down in her soul that spending time with Ryan was dangerous for her. She was simply too attracted to him, and that spelled danger with a capital D.

Darting a covert glance at his handsome profile, she felt her heart patter, her stomach tickle with that strange giddiness she knew was that all-too-human chemical reaction known as temptation.

Why now? she wondered. And why Ryan Shane? She simply didn't have an answer. She only knew she felt his allure. Only knew she recognized the threat of enticement. And being captivated by a man, any man, was not something she wanted. Not now. Not ever.

But, she'd already agreed to this bargain with Ryan. She was already in this mess. Up to her neck, it seemed.

Okay, just calm down, she told herself. You're a

grown woman. An intelligent human being. You can do this. You can keep your side of the arrangement and still protect yourself. The answer was simple really. All she needed to do was make certain Ryan understood that this deal of theirs had limits.

She looked over at his smooth, tanned features, saw how his blue gaze was focused with single-minded intent on the road ahead. Lord, but he was so good-looking. Why did the man have to be so darned gorgeous?

Clearing her throat, she steeled herself to speak. "Um...ah, Ryan?" she said, hating how she halted and stammered. "Would you mind if we, kind of, talked about this bargain we've made?"

He glanced her way, alarm obvious in his eyes. "You're not backing out, are you?"

"No," she assured him, and saw him visibly relax. "It's just that..." Her voice trailed. She tried again. "I'd like to, well, I'd like to...clarify the terms of the agreement."

"Clarify the terms," he repeated softly. Then he bobbed his head slowly up and down.

She could see his shoulders relax and realized that occupying his mind with something other than their imminent meeting with Cherry was doing wonders to melt the tension pent up inside him.

"That's probably a good idea," he went on. "That way, we'll both know what the other is expecting."

"Exactly," she stated. She was glad they were on the same wavelength about this.

Then an awkwardness crept over her, crawling across her skin like a hoard of slow-moving insects. She shivered. How was she to tell him she expected a hands-off policy where their fake relationship was concerned? Panic surged through her, seeming to come from nowhere as Julia decided she'd just have to bite the bullet and blurt out the truth. She simply wouldn't survive this farce with her pride intact if she had to suffer through the feel of his skin against hers, the taste of his lips, no matter how fake the intimacies might be.

Instantly her thoughts flashed back to the night he'd kissed her on the doorstep. His lips had been hot. Deliciously hot. And she'd dreamed about them every single night since. She just couldn't let something like that happen again.

Granted, she had been the one who had instigated the kiss. Demanded it of Ryan, actually. But she'd learned her lesson. Right then and there. The kiss had been a mistake. If she was to keep a clear head on her shoulders where this man was concerned, then their behavior toward one another had to have limits. Strict and firm limits.

"Well," she began. Then she paused to inhale slowly. "I know that I kind of, ah, forced you to kiss me the other night." She kept her eyes on the road ahead of them. "And I know that I explained my reason for, um, wanting that kiss. But I've, ah…"

Julia hated the choppy hesitation of her words. Hated the fact that voicing her thoughts was so difficult.

"I've decided," she continued, stronger now, "that our kissing was, um, a mistake."

He cut his eyes at her for only a split second, but she hadn't missed the silent questions in his gaze. He was obviously trying to figure out the meaning behind her statement. Well, she'd better come up with some further explanation, and fast, or Ryan might be quick to realize that his kiss had shaken her to the core.

"It was wrong of me," she hurried to say, "to put you on the spot like that. And I want you to know that

I won't be expecting that kind of..." She searched for the proper word. "Performance from you again."

"Aw, but Julia," he said, a quick grin evident in his tone, "that little bit of playacting was the best part of the evening. Didn't you think?"

Oh, yes. The silent, breathy answer flitted through her brain, and she barely stopped it from tumbling from her mouth. But she didn't dare voice those two tiny words. Doing so would only reveal the physical attraction she was feeling toward him. Besides, Ryan was teasing. That was more than obvious, and for some odd reason she felt saddened by the fact.

"Still," she said, a little louder than necessary, "I honestly think it would be best if we, ah, steered clear of any, you know, physical stuff."

A moment of tense silence hung between them, and then she steeled herself and faced him. Sensing her attention, he looked at her, his deep blue eyes glittering wickedly.

"Gee, Julia—"

His voice was soft as velvet and she felt it brush warm against her skin.

"I don't know if I like that rule."

A delicious shiver coursed down her spine. This man could oh, so easily turn on the boyish charm. If she wasn't teetering on the edge of a very dangerous precipice, she just might enjoy his gentle, sexy teasing. As it was, she felt an overwhelming need to slice through this sensual air he was creating with the blunt knife of reality.

"Look, Ryan," she said, keeping her tone flat and serious. "I'm only trying to clarify this...this *thing* we're getting involved in here, okay?"

"Okay, okay," he relented. He chuckled lightly. "I'm

sorry, Julia. It's just that it's so easy to get under your skin.''

Boy, she thought, he didn't know just how true that statement was!

"Yeah, well try to contain yourself. Let's keep our focus on the goal at hand.''

His tone grew serious as he said, ''So, no physical stuff.''

He shifted his hold on the steering wheel, obviously mulling over the thought.

"But,'' he suddenly said, ''how are we to convince Cherry or Kelly that there's anything between us if they never see us close?''

Julia realized this was a perfectly logical question. ''We'll just have to be convincing, that's all.'' Realizing this sounded lame, she floundered frantically until she came up with a clearer explanation. ''You know, we'll be verbally convincing. We'll toss little sweet nothings at one another. We'll call each other cute little names. That kind of thing.''

"That might work,'' he said, pondering the idea. Then he nodded. ''That's sure to work.'' He grinningly added, ''Sweetheart.''

The chuckle that escaped from her throat seemed to come from nowhere. Julia decided it was caused more by Ryan's syrupy tone rather than the nickname itself. Suddenly the atmosphere in the car turned light.

"Ryan,'' she admonished, ''you're going to have to sound a little more convincing than that.''

"Oh? How about this, *darling?*''

The silly emphasis he placed on the last word had her chuckling even harder. ''Nope,'' she told him. ''You still haven't got it.'' Then unable to fight the urge to try one of her own, she said, ''Snookums.''

They drove toward the north end of town, laughing all the way.

The apartment complex was brand new, a set of six identical concrete-and-glass structures that sported jutting angles and imaginatively hidden entrances to each unit. The style was much too contemporary for Julia's taste, however she remained silent and simply followed a suddenly quiet Ryan along the cement walkway.

"The door's ajar," he noted when they reached the empty apartment.

Julia nodded. "Maybe Cherry's waiting inside."

His deep blue eyes clouded over with dread. She wanted to reach out to him, to let him know they'd get through this. But she resisted the urge. *Limits,* she reminded herself.

"Come on," she said, hoping her light tone would soothe his apprehension. She pushed open the door and stepped inside, her gaze immediately drawn to the foyer's cathedral ceiling.

A boxy, crystal light fixture hung over them, and Julia could see down the hallway to the far end of the apartment where a huge window allowed a beautiful view of the city skyline.

"Wow," was all she could say.

Ryan only sighed heavily. His gaze darted about, but Julia easily determined his mind wasn't on his surroundings at all. Obviously he was searching for Cherry, feeling more than a little anxious about seeing the woman. For the first time Julia perceived the immense pressure he was under. The gorgeous redhead must be putting a great deal of effort into pursuing him.

Even though it was going against her better judgment,

she gave in to impulse, reached out and lightly touched his arm. "It's going to be okay," she assured him.

He didn't even seem to hear. "Let's get this over with," he murmured, and moved off toward the back of the spacious apartment. "Cherry?" he called.

"Oh, Ryan, isn't it great?"

The silky sensuality in Cherry's voice had Julia feeling like she wanted to cringe.

"I'm in the kitchen," Cherry said. "Come see. It's just perfect."

They passed through the huge living room with its wall of glass, and Julia paused to take in the full effect of the striking vista. With the towering buildings in the distance and the strategically planted trees in the foreground, the view was a pleasant mixture of both urban and rustic. She didn't want to begin to guess what the rent would be on this tiny rural oasis in the city.

"Psst."

Julia looked up and saw Ryan motioning her forward with a quick jerk of his head.

"Sorry," she whispered, and she hurried to catch up to him.

But she was too late.

Cherry came out of the kitchen and met Ryan in the doorway, planting a kiss square on the man's mouth.

"Isn't this place great," she purred softly to Ryan, completely ignorant of Julia's presence. Smoothing her palm lazily down the lapel of his jacket, Cherry said, "It's the perfect place for a couple just starting out."

In that instant, something strange and ugly took place inside of Julia. She couldn't figure out if it was the way Cherry had kissed Ryan, the familiar manner in which the woman was touching him, or the intimate inference in what she'd said. However, it *was* quite easy for Julia to figure out that she didn't like Cherry Richards. Didn't like her at all. And that thought took Julia by complete and utter surprise because she wasn't the kind of person who harbored feelings of aversion and hostility against anyone.

Why would Cherry Richards churn up such dark emotions in her? Julia wondered. She'd come into this situation knowing the woman wanted Ryan for her own. That was why she'd accompanied Ryan to Cherry's dinner. That was why she was here at this apartment right now. But witnessing Cherry's blatant possessiveness toward Ryan irritated Julia to no end.

Clearing her throat daintily to make her presence known, she was pleased to see a startled Cherry jump away from Ryan.

Oh, but the woman is good, Julia thought as she watched Cherry recover so quickly from her obvious astonishment.

"Well, hello," Cherry greeted smoothly. "I remember you from the other night at dinner." She offered her hand. "It's Julie, isn't it?"

"Julia, actually," Julia corrected.

Cherry's smile was cold, and the woman withdrew her hand from Julia's quickly, as if she were afraid of being tainted in some way by her touch. But that was perfectly fine with Julia.

"Ryan," Cherry said, "I didn't know you'd be bringing anyone along."

"I, uh…" Ryan began.

"Ryan told me you were scouting out some apartments for him," Julia said. "I invited myself along."

"Oh."

Cherry looked pleased…no, that expression could be described as nothing less than smug. And it was then that Julia realized her mistake. In telling Cherry that she'd asked to come along, Julia had all but relegated herself to Cherry's level—just another woman chasing Ryan. And it was clear from the look on Cherry's face that this was a battle the woman thought she could easily win.

Sidling up to Ryan, Cherry slid her long, lacquer-tipped fingers over his shoulder and sort of hung there at his side. She smiled up into his face.

"Yes, well," she said, "I told Daddy that I want to help Ryan out any way that I can."

"I do appreciate your effort." Ryan looked uncomfortable.

"Just wait until you see the master bedroom," Cherry said to him, her tone intimate. "It's gorgeous. The tub is big enough for two."

My Lord! Julia silently exclaimed. The woman's a hussy.

Ryan darted a glance at her and Julia could see he was about to panic. She needed to do something, and she needed to do it quick.

Instinct shouted at her to go over to Ryan, to take his hand, to lay some claim on him. But with Cherry draped over the man like a fox stole, Julia felt that such an action would come off as overkill. Besides, she thought, she'd already set the limits earlier in the car—limits that stipulated a hands-off approach.

Words were her only weapon against this she-devil, Julia realized, so she'd need to plan carefully and use her ammunition to her best advantage.

"The place is beautiful," she complimented Cherry.

Well done, she thought. Lull the enemy with praise.

"And, honey..." Julia lowered her voice to its sultriest level and directed it at Ryan. "Cherry's right. This apartment *is* big enough for two."

As in me and you, her eyes boldly suggested. She held his gaze for a long second before breaking the contact with a slow, discreet blink and then smiling ever so sweetly at Cherry. The redhead's face became shadowed with anger and she stepped away from Ryan. Julia doubted he noticed Cherry's expression. He was too busy staring mutely at her.

The atmosphere between the two women was so tense with aggression it could have been sliced with a saber. Julia knew Ryan needed saving from the female battle of wills and words that was surely about to begin.

"Ryan?" Her tone was louder than necessary.

He gave a subtle jerk at the sound of his name.

"Why don't you go have a look at the master suite?" Julia suggested. "And Cherry can show me the kitchen."

"Good idea," he murmured. Like a flash of lightning in a storm, he was gone.

The spiked heels of Cherry's pumps clicked on the tile floor of the kitchen. Julia followed her into the room, steeling herself for a verbal war.

"Lots of cabinet space," Julia remarked lightly.

"Yes, there certainly is." Running her fingers along the shiny countertop, Cherry bluntly remarked, "I was surprised to learn that Ryan is in a serious relationship."

"Oh?" Julia said, absently opening the door to the small pantry.

"I have to admit," Cherry said, "when you showed up at my dinner party with him, I thought you were just someone he'd…picked up on a whim."

Julia's spine stiffened. She reminded herself that it wasn't her intention to be rude to this woman, that she was only to do what she could to make Cherry lose interest in Ryan, but that didn't mean she had to put up with being insulted herself. She stared hard at Cherry, but remained silent.

"I didn't know the two of you were actually seeing one another on a regular basis," Cherry went on.

Choosing her words carefully, Julia was glad to discover she didn't need to lie. "Ryan and I are growing closer every day."

Let Cherry read into that what she liked, Julia mused. The woman didn't need to know that Julia felt her association with Ryan was a prickly situation that could very easily turn into a complicated mess.

"I've known him for years," the woman told her. "Ryan is a close family friend."

"I know." Julia ignored the emphasis Cherry had put on the word "close," and she turned to admire the gleaming, state-of-the-art stove.

"Ryan is very special to my father."

"I know that, too," Julia said, peeking inside the oven.

"And my father is doing all he can to get Ryan set up in his new practice."

Julia clearly heard the hidden messages. Ryan was right, she thought. Cherry is the kind of woman who will use every possible means to get what she wants.

Facing Cherry, Julia said, "I think it's a wonderful thing that Ryan has friends who are willing to help him."

"Oh, but Daddy and Ryan are much more than mere friends." Cherry's lips curled into a egotistic smile. "You could almost say that Daddy is Ryan's mentor. His—" she searched the air for the perfect term "—pseudo-father."

A smile tugged at Julia's mouth. "Then that makes you Ryan's pseudo-sister, doesn't it? No wonder you want to help him get settled into an apartment." Her smile widened as she plowed ahead innocently. "And that helps to clarify your relationship. Thanks for telling me. It puts my mind at ease."

Cherry glared, tucking her arms tightly under her rounded breasts. "Look, Julie—"

"Julia," she corrected softly but firmly.

"Whatever," Cherry said, her green eyes taking on the sudden ferociousness of a wild tiger. "You need to know something. I want Ryan. And I mean to have him."

Julia found Ryan in the master bedroom, and he turned to face her when she came into the room.

"Did I hear the front door close?" he asked softly.

She nodded. "Cherry just left."

His whole body seemed to relax at the news. The remaining tension left him in the form of a small, humorless chuckle.

"I'm surprised."

Julia shrugged. "She was pretty blunt when she said there was little use in her staying if I was here."

"She said that?"

"Yes," she told him. "And a lot more."

Ryan grimaced. "I'm sure." After a long minute, he sighed. "I thought you might have been the one who left," he said. "I pictured you running for your life."

She smiled at him. "I'm pretty good at digging in my heels."

Ryan ran his fingers through his tawny hair. "I wouldn't have blamed you, you know."

Julia knew she didn't need to respond.

"It is a nice apartment," Ryan ventured.

Again she nodded silently.

"It's a bit grand for me, though," he admitted. "I wonder what the rent is."

"Cherry said she'd call you with all the details."

He hissed an exhalation through clenched teeth. "Oh, I'm sure she will."

"And," Julia went on, "she said she'd stop in for lunch one day next week."

Ryan's head tipped up, his gaze steady on her face. "Did she mention which day she'd be coming?" he asked softly.

"She didn't say."

He groaned. "Knowing Cherry, it'll be every day."

"Hey, don't worry," Julia told him. "We can easily solve that problem."

Hope sparked in his deep blue eyes, and Julia felt her nerve endings tingle with pleasure knowing she'd put it there.

"Sure," she said. "I'll just pack us a sandwich and come to your office for lunch."

"Every day?" Absently he tucked his hand into the pocket of his trousers. "That won't be a bother?"

She hefted one shoulder a fraction. "If Cherry's going to be a threat during your lunch hours next week, then I'd say my coming to your office with a sandwich is part of our bargain, wouldn't you?"

Actually the prospect of spending the afternoons with Ryan had her feeling giddy with anticipation. But she'd never admit that out loud. In fact, she shouldn't allow herself to even think such a thing.

Ryan smiled at her then, and the giddiness jumping in her stomach calmed and heated and melted, spreading through her like warm, sweet jam. Before she realized what was happening, he'd closed the gap between them and gently placed his hands on her shoulders.

"Thanks, Julia," he said, his voice silky and intimate.

Hearing her name roll off his tongue in such a heart-felt, visceral manner ignited a fire in Julia.

"I'd have never gotten through today without you."

He was so close. Too close. The scent of his cologne wafted around her, his skin felt warm through the fabric of her top, and she felt as if time was running at half speed. She couldn't think. Couldn't breathe.

Slowly he let his hands slide down her arms.

"You were wonderful," he said. "I stood there looking like an idiot. But you took the situation in hand."

Limits. Remind him of the limits, her brain murmured silently. She found it easy to ignore the thought. His touch felt heavenly, smooth and warm against her flesh. Like a hot, satiny breeze blowing straight from a tropical paradise.

He chuckled, the sound rumbling from deep in his chest, and if Julia didn't feel completely frozen in place, she'd have lifted her fingers and placed them against his shirtfront where she could feel the vibration of his laugh.

"And I do want to thank you for getting me out of there when you did," he said. "Your timing couldn't have been more perfect."

Then he moistened his bottom lip, a quick and unconscious action, but the sight of it had her heart pounding, her blood pulsing, as her eyes riveted to his sexy mouth.

Step away from him, her brain ordered. But her feet wouldn't move. Her body refused to respond.

His strong fingers gently kneaded the muscles in her upper arms, and Julia dragged her gaze back up to his. Her whole body heated up, as if there were liquid fire spreading just under her skin, tiny flames licking and dancing over every inch of her. She felt her breath quicken, her chest rising and falling.

She pleaded with her limbs, her muscles, to contract, to expand, to *move*. But nothing happened. And again, she felt certain he was totally unaware of this full-fledged shutdown she was so torturously enduring.

"Tell me," Ryan said softly, "what did she have to say when the two of you were alone?"

He's waiting for a response. The words reverberated in her head, bouncing around in the frantic chaos of her brain.

Say something. Say something now!

"She, ah…" Julia heard the rusty sound of her voice and stopped. Her mouth was desert dry, and she wished fervently that she had something cool and wet to sip.

Lowering her lids, she took a moment to gather her wits about her. But she knew it was an attempt that would remain futile until she put a little space between herself and Ryan.

Somehow she found the strength to back away from him. And she was relieved to discover that she did so with no stiff, jerky movements that might alert him to the pandemonium reigning inside her.

"She made her feelings quite plain," Julia was able to say.

"Oh?"

She nodded, then swallowed. Every second of hesitation helped her to rally even more.

"She sees me as a small threat at best," she said. "Cherry is certain she has much more to offer you than I ever could. And she's bound and determined to have you."

Ryan reached up and massaged the back of his neck,

and she easily imagined those fingers smoothing across her own skin.

Stop! she commanded. Focus on the conversation!

"She actually told you that?" he asked.

He seemed incredulous that Cherry would be so bold. "Well, yes."

Ryan shook his head miserably, his hand falling back to his side. "Oh, boy, it's worse than I'd first imagined."

Having put a little distance between herself and Ryan, Julia felt her sanity slowly returning. Her thoughts came easier and more clearly.

"I wouldn't say it's worse," she told him. "But she is one determined woman."

"You can say that again," he muttered. An intense concern shone in his gaze. "How are we going to get out of this?"

She didn't miss his use of the plural pronoun, and a tiny thrill shivered through her.

"We're going to stick to the plan," she told him. "I'll be with you as often as possible when Cherry comes around. It might take some time, but she'll get the message. Eventually."

Ryan moved to gaze out the bedroom window, and Julia couldn't take her eyes off his handsome profile. She realized suddenly that she was going to be in deep trouble indeed if she didn't garner some kind of control over her reaction to this man.

After several silent moments Ryan turned to her. "I guess you're sorry I dragged you into this mess."

"No." Julia was afraid the tiny word was a lie, but then realized it was, and it wasn't. And that complicated thought scared her even more.

One corner of his mouth tipped up in a grin and Julia couldn't help but think it sexy.

"You have to agree," he said, "that this is one heck of a tangled web."

"Oh," she said softly, "I will agree with that." Even as the answer passed her lips, she helplessly realized the web they were weaving would only get more tangled with time.

He heaved a sigh. "I'm sorry."

"Oh, don't you dare apologize," she said. "You won't be getting off easy yourself, you know. Charlotte and I have parties to cater tonight and tomorrow, so I won't be free for a couple of days. But I'll be expecting you for dinner on Sunday." Julia couldn't stop the grin that crept across her lips. "And if you think Cherry is determined, just wait until you spend a little time with my teenage daughter."

Chapter Six

His lips skimmed across her bare shoulder like a deep, dark secret, tantalizing and irresistible, and Julia's breath caught in her throat. Their afternoon interlude had a shadowed, hazy feel, but the desire shining in Ryan's deep blue eyes was unmistakable. A desire that was hot and heady.

The pads of his fingertips were warm and smooth as he slowly trailed them down the length of her throat. His silky breath grazed her jaw as he hovered over her, and she closed her eyes, anticipating the feel of his mouth against hers—

"Mom."

The rude shove against Julia's shoulder had her blinking awake, and the soft and sensuous picture in her head dissolved. The romance novel she'd been reading slipped from its resting place on her abdomen to the bedspread.

A dream! She'd been dreaming. Of Ryan. Again.

"Mom, the timer went off in the kitchen." Kelly

crossed her arms. "And I didn't know if I was supposed
to take the chicken out of the oven or just baste it."

Julia's eyelids lowered, almost of their own volition,
and she realized she felt groggy and not a bit refreshed
by her impromptu nap. She'd worked hard over the past
couple of days.

"Mom?" There was impatience in Kelly's tone.
"You are awake, aren't you?"

"Yes, Kelly," she said, sitting up and planting her
feet on the floor. "I'm awake."

"You said you were coming up to have a bath." Kelly
shook her head in disapproval as she took a step away
from the bed. "And then you fall asleep. How can you
sleep when you have a date coming for dinner?"

Her daughter didn't let her respond before continuing
her tirade. "Do you realize he'll be here soon?"

For the first time Julia noticed the nervous anticipation
glittering in the child's dark eyes. She also noticed the
tailored red dress with its white buttons, and the strappy
white sandals on her daughter's feet.

"You look lovely," Julia remarked after looking her
up and down.

Kelly rolled her eyes. "Well, I can't have your boyfriend thinking I dress like a bum now, can I?"

"He's not my boyfriend." The words were out of her
mouth before she even realized it, and it sounded like
an overly emphasized protestation even to her. "Look,"
she began again, "Ryan and I are just spending a little
time together, is all. Let's not make more of it than there
is." She raked her fingers through her mop of hair.
"You wanted me to have some fun. And that's just what
I'm doing. Okay?"

For some odd reason, the dream she'd just had came
to mind with vivid clarity…dark and sexy images filled

with longing and passion, and Julia felt her skin grow warm with embarrassment.

Why would her subconscious plunk those visions and emotions in her head when she was most vulnerable? She and Ryan were *not* involved in any kind of permanent relationship. They had a deal. A bargain. Ryan was not her boyfriend.

She was just about to belabor that point when Kelly said, "Okay, already. So he's not your boyfriend. But I am glad he's coming to dinner. Now, do I take the chicken out of the oven, or do I baste."

"Baste," Julia said. "There's a saucepan with—"

"Butter and white wine basting sauce on the stove. I know. I know."

There was more eye rolling and Julia was forced to smile.

"I've lived with you all my life," Kelly told her. "I know how to herb-roast a chicken."

Kelly was at the door when she turned back to face her mother. "You'd better grab a quick shower," she said. "There's no time to lounge in the bathtub now." Her gaze zeroed in on Julia to get her full attention. "And please wear something nice."

"Yes, ma'am," Julia said, her dutiful tone tinged with good-natured sarcasm.

Once she was alone, Julia couldn't help feeling a little chagrined. Almost as though she was the child and Kelly the parent.

"So this is what life comes to," she muttered as she hurried to the bathroom.

Steamy water sluiced over her body in a fine spray, and she lathered her hair with shampoo. As she tilted her head back to rinse, the questions that had plagued her just a few minutes ago came back with a vengeance.

Why would her mind conjure such images of Ryan? she wondered. Granted, the man was gorgeous. But the two of them had no future. All he wanted from her was protection from another woman. And all she wanted from him was help in changing her image of a workaholic who didn't know how to have a good time. She shouldn't allow herself to be so attracted to the man.

On second thought, maybe she couldn't do much about this physiological attraction. But what was it that had her so intent on his physical attributes? Why was she dreaming about his handsome face, his charming smile, his broad shoulders, his magical hands, his great body, his heated kiss—

"Stop!" she commanded out loud. Then she murmured, "Get a grip, woman."

It wasn't as if she were some innocent eighteen-year-old with runaway hormones. She could take charge of her thoughts. Of course she could. She *would*. She simply needed to focus on what she wanted. A future free of entanglements with any man. She simply didn't want a "till death do us part" relationship. Not after what she'd endured during her teenage years....

The romance novels! The idea flashed into her brain just as she'd shut off the tap and reached for a towel. Those romance novels she read voraciously were the reason her libido was running amok.

Julia wrapped the towel around her body and reached for the blow-dryer, hating the idea that she'd have to stop indulging in her favorite pastime. She simply loved those stories of happily-ever-after. Lord knew, the only place a woman could find such a thing was between the pages of a good work of fiction. But she couldn't allow her passions to be stirred up. She just couldn't take any more sensuous dreams starring Ryan Shane.

Combing her fingers through her short, wavy locks, she made fast work of drying her hair.

She'd simply have to do away with her romance novels. At least until her deal with Ryan was completed and the man was out of her life. Heaving a sigh, she felt a little relieved to know she'd discovered the root of the problem—a root that could be yanked out of the garden of her world with very little effort. And with a lighter step, she set off toward her bedroom to dress for dinner.

Standing at Julia's front door, Ryan tugged at the collar of his shirt and then smoothed his fingers along one edge of the pink tissue paper surrounding the bouquet of fresh-cut daisies. The flowers were for Julia. She deserved every one of them for the way she'd taken care of his apartment-hunting dilemma last Friday. She'd been wonderful. Granted, Cherry hadn't given up her pursuit of him. In fact, she'd left several messages for him with Charlotte. Messages he hadn't gotten around to responding to yet.

He reached out, and pressed the buzzer and, glancing down at the flowers, pondered the hesitancy welling up inside him. Would Julia place more meaning on the flowers than a mere thank-you for a job well done? he wondered. Because that's all the flowers were meant to do. Show his appreciation for her efforts in getting rid of Cherry.

The daisies had no other meaning than that. None.

It was so very important to him that Julia not get the wrong idea about their relationship. He likened their agreement to a business arrangement. A safe, detached business arrangement. He simply couldn't allow it to develop into anything more than that.

He liked Julia. He thought she was a wonderful per-

Dear Reader,

Because you've chosen to read one of our fine romance novels, we'd like to say "thank you!" And, as a <u>special</u> way to thank you, we've selected <u>two more</u> of the books you love so well, <u>plus</u> an exciting mystery gift, to send you absolutely **FREE!**

Please enjoy them with our compliments...

Candy Lee

Editor

P.S. And because we <u>value</u> our customers, we've attached something extra inside...

FREE GIFT SEAL — EDITOR'S FREE GIFT SEAL THANK YOU

Peel off seal and Place inside...

How to validate your
Editor's FREE GIFT "Thank You"

1. Peel off gift seal from front cover. Place it in space provided at right. This automatically entitles you to receive two free books and a fabulous mystery gift.

2. Send back this card and you'll get brand-new Silhouette Romance™ novels. These books have a cover price of $3.50 each, but they are yours to keep absolutely free.

3. There's no catch. You're under no obligation to buy anything. We charge nothing—ZERO—for your first shipment. And you don't have to make any minimum number of purchases—not even one!

4. The fact is thousands of readers enjoy receiving books by mail from the Silhouette Reader Service™. They like the convenience of home delivery...they like getting the best new novels BEFORE they're available in stores... and they love our discount prices!

5. We hope that after receiving your free books you'll want to remain a subscriber. But the choice is yours— to continue or cancel, any time at all! So why not take us up on our invitation, with no risk of any kind. You'll be glad you did!

6. Don't forget to detach your FREE BOOKMARK. And remember...just for validating your Editor's Free Gift Offer, we'll send you THREE gifts, *ABSOLUTELY FREE!*

GET A FREE MYSTERY GIFT...

YOURS FREE!

SURPRISE MYSTERY GIFT COULD BE YOURS _FREE_ AS A SPECIAL "THANK YOU" FROM THE EDITORS OF SILHOUETTE

son. He didn't want to end up seeing her hurt. And he didn't want to be hurt himself.

In his line of work, every day he watched previously devoted couples tear each other apart. And being the lawyer for one or the other, he actually felt that he lent a helping hand to all that pain. Over the years he'd learned to detach himself from all the bickering and feuding, and he did what he could to get his clients and their children into some kind of counseling. But he had no desire whatsoever to personally endure such an experience.

Sure, he and Julia were not married. They would not have to suffer through a divorce. But he couldn't help but feel that any relationship between a man and a woman would eventually break up, and the split would be filled with hurtful words and angry regrets. He didn't need that kind of aggravation.

Reaching for the buzzer a second time, he saw the door being pulled open and he drew back his hand.

"Hi."

He smiled. "Hello," he said. He'd met Kelly before, yet he couldn't help but marvel at just how much the teen looked like her mother with her large, inky eyes and her wavy, midnight hair cut in that cute style.

"Come on in," Kelly said, opening the door. "Mom's still getting ready."

He was ushered into the living room. "Something smells good," he said.

"Dinner." Kelly smiled.

The room provided the perfect image of hearth and home with its dainty throw pillows and soft, inviting furniture. The delicious aroma only heightened the "family" feel of the room.

Panic made his mouth go dry. He couldn't let Julia

get the wrong idea about these flowers. He didn't want to be the cause of even one instant of pain coming into this peaceful place. With his thoughts in a sudden frenzy, he thrust the bouquet at Kelly.

"Here," he said. "These are for you."

He could see that his abrupt tone and jerky movement had startled the teenager. Putting her at ease suddenly seemed vital.

"Really," he told her, his voice softening, "I hope you like them."

When she blinked slowly, her dark lashes fanned across her skin. And then her gaze glittered with pure pleasure.

"Thank you." She drew the flowers gently to her chest. "No one's ever given me flowers before."

A flash of royal blue had him glancing toward the doorway. His eyes locked onto Julia, and his heart kicked against his ribs. She was beautiful. The fabric of her dress hugged her shoulders and the roundness of her breasts, but once it reached her waist, the material fell in soft folds to mid-calf.

"Wow." He was helpless to keep the word from passing across his lips. "You look great."

Her wide smile had his blood pounding.

"Thank you, Ryan," she said.

Her voice wrapped around him like warm velvet, and he frowned. What was the matter with him? He'd acknowledged from the very beginning that Julia was a beautiful woman. With her midnight eyes and her sassy black hair, any man would come to that conclusion. Yet he'd lectured himself over and over about allowing himself to actually react to her physical attributes.

"I need to check on dinner," Julia said to him.

"Kelly, would you mind keeping Ryan company for a few minutes?"

Instantly, Kelly offered, "I'll go. That way you can stay here and visit."

Something akin to panic flashed across Julia's face, intriguing Ryan and taking his mind off of the silent rebuke he was giving himself.

"Why don't we all just go into the kitchen?" Julia suggested, her tone stiff and abrupt. "That way, we can check on dinner, and…and we can get Ryan a nice glass of lemonade."

Her smile was meant to cover the brusqueness of her manner, but it didn't quite work. If Ryan didn't know better, he'd think she didn't want to be alone with him. But of course he did know better.

"Sure," he said, feeling the small crease of bewilderment knitting his brow.

Kelly looked from one of them to the other. She shrugged and then traipsed off toward the back of the house. Julia and Ryan followed in silence.

"Have a seat, Ryan," Julia said, indicating a stool at the small butcher-block island in the middle of the floor. "Kelly, pour him a glass of lemonade, please."

"Sure thing." Kelly moved automatically to the refrigerator and pulled out a glass pitcher.

The savory smell of onions and herbs and roasted chicken was even stronger now. When Julia opened the oven door and bent to check on the chicken, Ryan's gaze followed the line of her body until his eyes rested on the blue-clad curve of her fanny. His mouth watered.

Stop it! he commanded, his throat muscles convulsing in a swallow. But how could he stop noticing Julia when every inch of her was so damned noticeable?

With his eyes still glued to her derriere, he silently

blamed the cooking aromas wafting into the room for his unsettling reaction, and although he knew it was a barefaced lie, he latched onto the excuse and believed it with all his might. To do otherwise would demand that he look more closely at the implications of—

"Here you go."

Forced to look up at Kelly when she plunked a tall glass in front of him, Ryan saw the glimmer of knowing in the teen's eye.

Oh, Lord, he thought. She knows I'm ogling her mother. Suddenly he felt his face flush with heat, but thankfully the teenager had turned her back on him. She picked up a knife and chopped several cloves of garlic. Ryan identified the herb by its intense scent.

"Everything smells great," he said, desperate to fill the empty space hanging in the air.

Julia set the roasting pan on the island between them and then she spooned the pan drippings over the bird's golden skin.

"We're having chicken," Julia said. "Fresh sweet peas, smashed potatoes and fresh rolls."

Curiosity had Ryan's brows raising. "*Smashed* potatoes?"

"Yeah," Julia told him. "They're Kelly's favorite."

"We cook garlic in some butter," Kelly piped up, "and then we add the hot potatoes, a little light cream, a sprinkling of salt and pepper, and some rosemary."

The teen glanced at him over her shoulder. "Then we just smash 'em a little. Not until they're smooth." She grinned. "I like 'em lumpy."

"I'd rather you say they have texture, Kelly," Julia remarked, grinning.

Ryan found it amazing just how much mother and daughter looked alike. And seeing Kelly, he decided Julia must have been a beauty when she was a teenager. "Sounds delicious," he said.

"Believe me, they are." Kelly turned back to her chopping.

Julia placed the chicken on a meat platter. "He doesn't have to believe you. If we can get dinner on the table, he can taste for himself."

The burst of lemon that exploded on his tongue when he took a sip from the glass told him the juice was obviously homemade. Then he took another gulp, hoping the cool, tart-sweet tang would wash away the disconcertion knotting in his stomach. But it didn't, and he felt obliged to try to discover what caused the disturbing emotion.

He took in the scene before him, mother and daughter working together like a team to prepare a meal, heard their laughter—got caught up in it, actually. And like an unexpected hammer blow against the thumb, the love permeating the room pierced him to the bone. He felt the unmistakable homeliness of it all. And worse yet, he liked it.

All at once, Ryan felt he just might be in trouble.

Julia was in heaven. The chicken had been juicy, the potatoes flavorful with just the right hint of herb. The rolls had been tender and flaky. And her three layered chocolate cake had been decadently delicious. The best part about it was that Ryan had enjoyed every mouthful.

There was nothing more satisfying than serving a perfectly prepared meal. She and Kelly had planned, shopped for and prepared the food with great care. And they'd had fun doing the cooking together.

Sure, Kelly often helped prepare the catered food cooked for customers, but that was usually done in Charlotte's large kitchen. Cooking this meal for Ryan in their own smaller, more intimate kitchen had forced Julia and Kelly to communicate a little more. The close confines had even attributed to some funny situations, one of which had been when she'd tasted the gravy and Kelly had bumped her arm sending a rivulet of brown liquid dripping down Julia's chin.

The afternoon had been full of fun, and Julia made a mental note that she'd have to plan more elaborate meals a little more often. She and Kelly could use more carefree moments together.

Her eyes roved over the cluttered table, the dirty dishes, the wrinkled napkins, the warm and caring company. The conversation became a buzz in her ear as she studied first Kelly and then Ryan.

She couldn't help but marvel yet again about just how blue his eyes were. Julia knew she was attracted to him. She'd analyzed that problem, faced it head-on, and had come to the conclusion that she didn't want the entanglements of a relationship cluttering up her life. Besides, Ryan wasn't interested in her as a woman. And that only made it easier for Julia to keep her hormones in check.

But seeing him in this extremely familiar setting only seemed to heighten her attraction to him. It was…strange.

She sipped her after-dinner coffee and watched Kelly's eyes dance merrily as she related some story to Ryan. He was so absorbed by Kelly's conversation, Julia felt her heart warm. Her daughter had never had this kind of attention from a man.

Seemingly out of the clear blue, the phrase "fantasy father figure" flitted across Julia's brain. It so startled her that she jerked forward, sloshing coffee onto the white linen tablecloth.

"Are you okay?" Kelly asked.

"Did you burn yourself?"

There was deep concern in Ryan's eyes as he dabbed at the coffee stain.

"N-no," Julia sputtered, wiping at her mouth with an oversize linen napkin. "I'm okay," she assured them both. Then she pushed back her chair and stood. "Excuse me a moment."

Ryan replied, but Julia was in such a rush to get to the powder room she didn't hear him.

She pressed her back against the closed door and gulped in air, trying to calm her racing heart. She hadn't thought about her "fantasy father" for years. Since she was a preteen. Younger than Kelly is now.

Her real father had been so—

Placing her palms flat against her cheeks, she shook the image from her mind. She couldn't even begin to remember the man without tears welling up in her eyes.

Moving to the sink, she turned on the faucet, moistened her fingertips and gently dabbed at her forehead and cheeks with the cool water.

The fantasy father she'd conjured as a child had been a survival technique of sorts. When daily life with her dad became unbearable, Julia would closet herself in her room and add to the list of loving characteristics of her dream parent.

Seeing Kelly with Ryan, the child's eyes all bright with what could easily be described as adoration, had stirred the deepest recesses of Julia's memory. She'd prayed for a father who would listen rather than lecture. She'd wished for a father whose heart would be filled with love rather than anger and accusation.

"Stop," she murmured. Gripping the edge of the

white porcelain sink, she frowned into the mirror. "Stop thinking about him."

Kelly had never known her grandfather, Julia's father. Thank the Lord in heaven for that. Unfortunately, Kelly had also never known her own father, either. And that, Julia regretted. But there had been nothing she could do about it.

Just put the whole awful mess out of your head, Julia told herself. It's all in the past. Nothing can change the past.

She inhaled deeply, absently smoothing her fingers over her hair.

"The past is all just bad memories anyway," she reminded herself softly. "Bad memories that don't even deserve to be remembered."

Julia moistened her lips and squared her shoulders, feeling strong enough now to go back into the dining room and entertain Ryan.

This evening might have summoned some old memories, but Ryan's visit had accomplished some good. She'd recaptured a closeness with Kelly as they had shopped and cooked Ryan's meal, and her daughter's smile was free and open when it was directed at her. Yes, her "date" with Ryan had achieved something. With a new resolve, Julia pulled open the door and flipped off the light.

She was smiling as she went down the hallway. But she stopped in the dining room doorway, sensing a heavy, serious feel in the air.

"You know," Ryan was saying softly, "if you want me to, maybe I could talk to her."

"Oh, would you?"

A crease bit into Julia's brow as she heard the puppy-like appreciation in her daughter's question.

"Talk to me about what?" Julia asked.

They swiveled to face her, both of them looking as if they'd gotten caught with their fingers in the proverbial cookie jar.

Chapter Seven

Kelly studied the ice cubes in the bottom of her empty glass, her head sunk low between her shoulders. Ryan's eyes were still on Julia's face, but his gaze had grown hooded. And the fact that he remained stone silent told her he wasn't quite sure how to broach what must be the difficult topic at hand.

Julia decided she had two options, she could focus on Ryan and let her daughter lay low during the coming discussion, as Kelly apparently desired, or she could dive right in and involve everyone present.

The second option, she decided, was the healthier one. If Kelly had a subject she wanted to talk about, then the child needed to know she had to fight her own battles.

Fight her own battles? Julia frowned, wondering why she felt war was on the horizon. Glancing at Kelly's rounded shoulders and then at Ryan's shrouded expression, she nodded. Yes, conflict was most definitely in the air.

"Kelly," she said, easing down into her chair, "we've

always been able to talk about anything. If you have something you want to say to me, you don't need Ryan to talk for you."

Her daughter refused to meet her eyes.

"Come on, now," Julia urged. "You know you can say whatever's on your mind."

Without lifting her head, Kelly muttered, "No, I can't."

"Of course you can. What is it? What's on your mind?"

Silence.

"Kelly, look at me."

When she did as she was told, the child's eyes were so flat with resentment that Julia was sorry she'd made the order. Then she directed her gaze at Ryan, wondering what he must be thinking.

Having lived in a house with a teenager, Julia knew how quickly the weather could change from sunshine to rain—complete with thunder and lightning—in the blink of an eye. One moment the atmosphere could be full of frolic and giggles, and the next could be fraught with angry words and bitter tears. These shifts were simply taken for granted as a parent. However, for someone like Ryan, someone who had little-to-no experience with kids, the sudden bends and twists of her daughter's emotions could be extremely disconcerting to say the least.

When Julia had left the room, Kelly had been sharing a lively conversation with Ryan. Now her daughter's aura felt dark with anger. Ryan must be totally confused by the metamorphosis.

She wanted to assure him that this was normal. That all teens had their ups and downs. But to voice that opinion right now would come off as condescending to

Kelly. Julia knew her first concern at the moment should be her daughter.

Before Julia could speak, however, Kelly slid out of her chair and made to stand. Julia stopped her by placing her hand on the child's forearm.

"Don't, Kelly," she said, forcing her voice to remain soft. "We can't solve anything if you run away. We can only fix things if we talk."

Kelly eased her weight back onto the seat of the chair, but she stayed perched right on its edge. Then she pulled her arm out of her mother's grasp, and Julia let go. Resisting Kelly's need for space would be a mistake right now, Julia decided. Her daughter would flee at the least provocation.

Maybe now wasn't the time for them to talk. Julia tucked her bottom lip between her teeth. Maybe she should wait until Ryan left and she and Kelly were alone.

But her daughter had been the one to involve Ryan in this. Whatever this was.

"Julia..."

The sound of Ryan's voice drew her eyes to his face.

"Kelly does want to talk." Then he looked at Kelly. "It's going to be okay."

Julia saw her daughter give Ryan a tiny, grateful smile, and her gut twisted with some dark, unnamable emotion. How dare Ryan take it upon himself to assure Kelly? And how dare Kelly accept his comfort? What were they doing? Ganging up on her?

With her sight glazing over with a sudden red haze, Julia felt her body grow hot, her heart pound.

"Look, Kelly," she said. "I don't know what's going on, or what it is you want to discuss with me, but I do have to tell you that I resent the fact that you used my absence to paint me as some sort of close-minded monster. I don't know what you said to Ryan—''

"Now, Julia," Ryan said, "Kelly did no such thing."

Ignoring him completely, Julia said, "Haven't I always been there for you, Kelly? Haven't we always been able to talk? Has there ever been a time when we couldn't work out our differences?" With the barest hesitation, she continued, "Let me answer for you. Yes. Yes. And no."

Julia felt swallowed by the angry fog, and when Ryan reached out and touched her hand, his fingertips felt cool against her hot skin.

"Why don't you let Kelly talk?" Ryan asked.

His question only fanned the flames of her fury. "Ryan, haven't I been sitting here trying to get her to say what's on her mind? Haven't I prodded her with questions?"

"Yes," Ryan allowed. "But you've also answered most of them for her."

Julia sat up straight, her jaw clamping shut. Ryan was right. She was talking at Kelly. Not to her.

She'd always prided herself on being a loving mother. On being open and accessible to Kelly. But she certainly hadn't been tonight, and she couldn't help but wonder why.

Like a jolt from an electric prod, she realized the answer. Ryan. Julia could hardly believe it, but she was actually jealous of the closeness Ryan was sharing with her daughter.

"I'm sorry," she said to them both. "I'll be quiet and listen." And then she focused all her attention on Kelly.

A thick and heavy silence weighed down the air, and finally Ryan reached across the table and gently took hold of Kelly's hand.

"Kelly," he said, "tell your mom what you told me."

Julia let her gaze slide down her daughter's arm to where Kelly and Ryan's fingers touched. And then she looked at her own hand, the one that Ryan had covered with his own.

A link. Ryan was acting like a link between herself and Kelly. She didn't know how she felt about that, didn't have time to ponder the concept.

"Mom..."

Remaining utterly still, Julia put all her effort into listening.

"I, um..." Kelly paused to swallow. "I have a boyfriend."

Julia felt a tremble run through her. It was a totally involuntary reaction. Ryan must have felt it because his fingers tightened over her hand.

"And I want to know," Kelly continued, "if...if I can invite Tyler to dinner. I want you to meet him."

Instinctively, Julia pulled her hands into her lap. Away from Ryan. She couldn't think straight with him touching her.

"You're kidding, right?" she asked. "There's no way you can be serious with this."

"Wait a minute," Ryan said to her. "Maybe it would be good if you were to meet Kelly's friend."

The glare she tossed at Ryan silenced him. Emotions bombarded her, one after another. Too many to decipher. She leveled her eyes onto Kelly. "Is this the same boy you sneaked out to be with?"

There was no need for Kelly to answer the question, her expression said it all. Julia twisted the napkin in her lap into tiny, tight circles. "Do you honestly expect me to invite this boy into our home? Prepare him a meal? Share cordial conversation with him? When I know you and he lied to me? When I know the two of you schemed and planned behind my back?''

Her tone was calm. Deceptively so. Inside, Julia felt like someone had tossed a match into a roomful of explosives.

"*We* did not plan anything!" Kelly pushed herself to a stand with such force that the chair rocked back onto its two hind legs. "He didn't know I sneaked out. He thought I had your permission to go to the movies. I told you that! But you don't believe anything I say."

Kelly raced from the room, and Julia heard her footsteps as she tromped up the stairs, then the slamming of her bedroom door.

The dining room was eerily silent. Looking down, Julia saw that she'd all but ruined the dinner napkin, it was twisted so tightly. She inhaled a deep and shaky breath to try to calm her twittering nerves.

"I'm sorry, Julia."

She gave him a half smile.

"It's all my fault," he said. "I was only trying to make conversation while you were out of the room. I asked her if she had a boyfriend. I had no idea my simple question would—" his brow creased "—ruin the evening."

"There was no way for you to know," Julia told him.

After a moment, Ryan said, "Gee, Kelly really sneaked out of the house?"

"Mmm-hmm. Ladder. Lies. The works." Julia felt the familiar ache of betrayal in her heart.

"You know, it isn't my place to say, but maybe you should meet this Tyler. It seemed awfully important to Kelly."

Julia's shoulders tensed. "She's fourteen years old,

Ryan. Everything is *awfully important* to her. And you're right, it isn't your place to say."

Ryan's startled silence made her realize just how callous and mean her words were.

"Look, I'm sorry," she said, absently combing her fingers through her hair. "I didn't mean that the way it sounded. I love my daughter. I love her dearly. But you have to understand that, to a teenager, everything holds life-and-death proportions."

He didn't look convinced, so she elaborated. "For example, yesterday morning Kelly wanted to wear her favorite T-shirt, but it wasn't clean. My daughter shed real tears and proclaimed that she'd just die if she didn't get to wear the shirt." Julia grimaced. "Needless to say, I did a load of laundry before I went to cook at Charlotte's."

Ryan glanced down into his cup of cold coffee.

"And just last week," Julia continued evenly, "Kelly promised me she'd love me for the rest of her entire life if I'd buy her her favorite rock band's CD. I bought it. But I don't think her promise is holding up too well."

Her last statement drew Ryan's gaze, and Julia smiled.

"Look," she said, leaning toward him, "I'm just trying to make you understand that I go through this kind of thing with Kelly on a daily basis. An hour from now she'll be fine. She'll forget all about this."

He shook his head. "I think you're wrong on this one."

"Oh?"

"I feel that Kelly really wants you to meet this boy. I think it's important to her. More important than any T-shirt or CD."

Ryan was merely voicing his opinion, Julia knew that.

But she also knew that behind his words, he was attacking her mothering techniques.

"Oh, yeah?" she said, the words passing her lips before her brain kicked in to stop them. "So tell me...who died and left you parent of the year?"

He was silent a moment, his blue eyes clouding with insult. Julia wanted to apologize—it had been such a stupid thing to say—but she couldn't get her tongue to form the words.

"You're right," he finally said. "I don't know a thing about bringing kids up in this world, so maybe I should just shut up about it."

"Maybe you should," she agreed.

"Maybe I should go, too."

She nodded once. "Maybe you should."

They both stood and headed for the front door.

"Why won't you meet Kelly's friend, Julia? Why won't you invite him into your home, sit him down, get to know him? Kelly's not asking for much."

Julia slipped in front of him and opened the front door. "Because she's fourteen years old, Ryan! She's too young to have serious boyfriends. I won't encourage that kind of behavior in my daughter."

"Like you said," he told her, "she's fourteen. Everything is life and death. She'll probably have twenty *serious* boyfriends before she graduates high school. That's what being a teenager is all about. Don't you remember what it was like?"

She felt as though she was holding on to her sanity by her fingernails. She wanted this man out of her house. Out of her sight. "I thought you were going to shut up about it."

"Fine," he said. He pushed open the screen door. "Tell Kelly I said goodbye."

"I will."

His clipped tone never wavered as he asked, "Are we still on for lunch tomorrow? Cherry will probably be coming into the office."

"I'll be there," Julia told him.

"Fine."

He turned and walked away, without looking back. And Julia closed the door before he even got to the bottom of the porch steps.

The elevator doors whooshed open and Julia stepped out onto the fifth floor of the building where Ryan rented office space. The wide hallway was carpeted in a plush dove gray, a calming color that set off the burgundy, pattern-papered walls with just the right amount of professionalism and understated charm. Ryan had made a great choice in business location.

Ryan L. Shane, Esq. Julia read the door plate and wondered what the "L" in Ryan's name stood for. Darn it! She shouldn't care a fig what the man's middle name was.

Hitching the picnic basket she carried higher onto her forearm, she reached for the heavy doorknob, a rush of anticipation coursing through her. Julia froze. What was wrong with her? This thrill she was feeling at the prospect of having lunch with Ryan was...dangerous.

He had no personal interest in her, she silently lectured. He was a man, and she knew from past experience that men only hurt the women in their lives. She'd seen that for herself. Witnessed it firsthand.

Besides that, Ryan had butted into her relationship with Kelly. He was opinionated. And his opinions directly opposed her own where raising her daughter was concerned.

She searched through her consciousness, trying hard to conjure the irritation she'd felt last night when Ryan had been at her house for dinner. Remembering their disagreement would be the perfect ammunition to battle these other, much too personal, feelings that were invading her mind.

The outer office of Ryan's suite smelled of fresh paint. There was an empty desk, and Julia knew he was looking into hiring a secretary.

She heard muffled voices coming from the inner office, one of them silky and feminine.

So Cherry had already arrived.

Moving closer to the door, Julia had every intention of bursting right in on the scene, but something in the tone of Cherry's voice stopped her.

"I'm only trying to tell you that there's no way that woman feels anything for you, Ryan," Julia heard Cherry say.

"I don't want to discuss this," Ryan said. "I'm not comfortable talking to you about my relationship with Julia."

Hearing that she was the topic of conversation, Julia's mouth went cotton dry.

"I'm your friend, aren't I?"

Cherry's question was purred more than it was spoken, and Julia felt her stomach pinch with disgust.

"Of course you are," Ryan said.

"And Daddy just wouldn't forgive me if I didn't tell you the honest-to-goodness truth—"

"What does Jim have to do with this?" His tone became sharp with concern.

"Well, Ryan," Cherry simpered, "you know I discuss everything with Daddy. And he agrees with me. Julia's a cold fish. She's just not capable of deep emotions."

Julia stifled a gasp. A cold fish? Where did Cherry get off saying—

"How did you come to *that* conclusion?"

Maybe Ryan wasn't refuting Cherry's description as fervently as Julia might like, but at least there was a healthy dose of bewilderment in his question.

"It was pretty easy, actually," Cherry answered. "Lovers share longing looks. Lovers take every opportunity to touch. To kiss. Julia has never so much as taken your hand, let alone kissed you."

Julia's heart hammered in her chest. Why hadn't she realized that the "hand's off" rule she'd insisted upon would get them into trouble in the end? She hadn't thought it out clearly because she'd been too intent on keeping her physical distance from Ryan.

"Well...now—"

Ryan sounded as if he was actually squirming under the pressure of Cherry's accusation.

"Maybe it's just that Julia doesn't like to be demonstrative in public."

Julia hated the fact that he felt the need to make excuses for her. She also hated the fact that the beautiful and sultry Cherry Richards, with her sexy tumble of red hair and her paper-white skin, with her flame-colored nails and her tight-fitting skirts, thought Julia was somehow less of a woman because she didn't lay all over Ryan every time they happened to have an audience.

Well, Julia had news for Cherry. She could be just as provocative, just as affectionate, as anyone. More even!

"Ryan," she heard Cherry say, "you know there are women available who are just waiting to give you just what you need."

That's it! That silky purr was back in Cherry's voice and it caused something inside Julia to snap.

There are women available, indeed! she grumbled silently. *Woman* is what Cherry means. And Cherry *is* that woman. The brazen hussy was offering herself up on a silver platter right there in Ryan's office.

Well, sugar, Julia whispered under her breath, you won't be taking *my* man.

Pushing the door open wide with her free hand, she waltzed into the office as if she owned the place.

"Hello, sweetheart." She locked her gaze onto Ryan as if he was the last man on earth. "I brought us a romantic little lunch for two, just like I promised."

Even though Julia knew Ryan had been expecting her, he looked totally taken by surprise by her entrance, and she almost chuckled. Totally ignoring Cherry, Julia placed the picnic basket on the desktop, rounded the desk and slid her arms up and around Ryan's neck. She pulled herself up on her toes until their faces were a scant inch apart.

"How's your day going, darling?" she whispered in a voice she hoped was effusive with seduction. It had been so long since she'd tried to be sexy, she had no idea if she could pull it off.

He didn't answer her right away, and his hesitation spurred a completely spontaneous and deviously delicious idea.

To hell with the hands-off rule! She moistened her lips, knowing without a doubt that what this situation called for was a kiss. And not just any kiss, either, she quickly decided, but a *possessive* kiss.

The tiny triangle of her pink tongue skimmed along her luscious lips, and Ryan was mesmerized by the sight. He had no idea what had gotten into Julia. Her sexy greeting. That for-your-eyes-only smile she was giving him. That midnight-temptress gaze.

And if he didn't know better...why...was she actually going to—

His breath stopped short, his eyes widened, as she pressed her mouth to his.

Hot. Honey-sweet. Paralyzingly powerful.

The words and phrases discharged in his brain like sparks flying from short-circuited wires.

He slid his arms around her and closed his eyes, reveling in the smell of her, the taste of her, the feel of her. He'd wanted this for so long. And now she was in his arms.

She parted her moist lips and slowly, tentatively, tasted him. Ryan felt a surge of desire rocket through him. He pulled her tightly against him and deepened the kiss, their tongues swaying and gliding in an age-old dance.

His thinking became fuzzy with the fiery passion burning deep in his gut. And the sound of her ragged breathing had his heart jackhammering in his chest. Or was that his breathing that was grating like a piece of rusty machinery?

Through the fog of purely carnal lust, Ryan slowly became cognizant of some...sound. Some irritating intrusion that refused to be ignored.

Not quite ready to pull away from Julia physically, Ryan mentally gathered his wits about him to discern what it was that was fighting for his attention. The sound of someone clearing their throat broke through the hazy stupor that held him captive.

Cherry!

Simply thinking the name was like a bucket of cold

water flung on the embers burning inside him. He'd forgotten all about Cherry.

He broke off the kiss so suddenly that he felt the need to grasp Julia's forearms to keep her from losing her balance. Ryan glanced down at Julia's face. Her cheeks were flushed, her lips moist and lusciously puffy. But it was the utter surprise in her dark eyes that fascinated him. Obviously, Julia had been as affected by the kiss as he—and she was shocked by that fact. Her expression was revealing; the wide gaze, the silent ''oh'' formed by her mouth.

He had a sudden urge to shout joyfully, to pick Julia up and swing her around in a tight little circle. But he didn't.

''Ah, honey,'' he said when he finally found his voice, ''Cherry's here.''

''Oh.'' This time the tiny word was spoken out loud.

Julia glanced over at Cherry, her face beaming with a smile lit with pure pleasure. ''Hello,'' she greeted silkily. ''Sorry about that little affectionate display.'' She darted a mock demure smile up at Ryan, and then her gaze returned to Cherry. ''But I thought we were alone.''

''Affectionate display?'' Cherry muttered. ''I thought the two of you were going to eat one another for lunch.''

''Ah,'' Julia said, ''speaking of lunch. Cherry won't you join us? I'm not sure I brought enough, but we could make do.''

The invitation was so blatantly uninviting that Ryan nearly laughed out loud.

''No, thank you,'' Cherry said, picking up her leather purse and tucking it under her arm. ''I was just leaving.''

Even though he was feeling overwhelmingly confused by Julia's behavior, Ryan could tell Cherry was livid. She smiled when she looked at him, but the expression didn't reach her cool green gaze. "I'll call you. I found a couple more apartments for you to look at."

And she was gone.

Ryan was still looking at the empty doorway when he felt a weight on his chest, tipping him off balance. He plopped onto his chair and his eyes widened when Julia sat on his lap.

"Was that good, or what?" she asked, snaking her arms around his neck.

Did she really have to ask? He'd been dreaming of kissing her like that for ages, and now that he had, nothing he'd imagined had even come close to reality.

"It was good," he answered, astounded and a little bewildered that she could talk so easily about what had just happened between them.

There was a smile on her beautiful face, and even though he felt reluctant to say or do anything that might make it disappear, he simply had to figure out what was going on.

"Julia. Ah…" he began slowly. "I, ah, I thought you were angry with me."

Her dark eyes were still bright with pleasure. "Oh, you mean about Kelly?" Julia shrugged. "No," she said. "Kelly was fine this morning. A little quiet maybe, but everything's going to be all right. I told you. She's a teenager. She gets over things quick."

Thoughts of Kelly had tweaked Ryan's conscience all night. He was worried that Julia needed to take her daughter's concerns a little more seriously. He wanted to talk to Julia about that, but he couldn't right now. Something else was weighing on his mind. That kiss.

"Well, ah, well…" He couldn't quite get beyond the awkwardness of his question. "What about the hands-off rule?"

In other words, what the hell just happened here? his mind shouted.

"You know," Julia said, "I thought about the rule. Really, I did. But when I heard what that woman was saying about me, I just couldn't take it." She slid her palms down the lapels of his suit jacket. "She called me a cold fish, Ryan. A cold fish!"

Julia's words spilled from her quickly, and Ryan found himself studying her face, taking in the meaning.

"Well, I showed her," Julia said, a smug smile playing across her lips. "I can be as much of a sexy siren—"

As she said the words, she swiveled her shoulders, and the simple laws of physics had her hips grinding gently on his lap. Ryan would have loved to be able to enjoy the sensation, but he was too damned busy trying to sort out all the details.

"As Miss Cherry." Julia grinned at him. "Can't I?"

He blinked once, twice. "You knew she was here."

It was a plain, unadulterated statement. Made the instant the thought formed in his head.

Julia had been playacting the whole time.

Of course, she was playacting, you idiot, his brain silently grated at him. *What did you think? That she wanted to kiss you? Wanted to call you darling? Wanted to flash those sexy black eyes at you?*

She was doing all that for Cherry's benefit.

"Of course," he murmured.

Her smile dimmed. "What?"

"Of course," he repeated, increasing the volume of his tone, "you were a sexy siren. A damn good sexy siren."

"Why, thank you," she said.

Her gratitude was genuine, and Ryan felt his chest constrict with pleasure at the sight of it. But there was disappointment there, too. And it lay in his gut like a heavy brick.

Julia stood, reached across the desk and pulled the picnic basket to her.

"You know," she said, pulling sandwiches and bottles of light-colored juice from the basket, "I've just now discovered something."

She was still close enough to him that her kneecap grazed the side of his leg. Ryan found himself focusing on the creamy skin exposed by her short skirt as he sorted through the confusion roiling inside him, as he dealt with the disappointment and desire churning in his blood.

When she placed the cold bottle of juice in his hand, the icy condensation helped him shove aside the quagmire of his emotions.

"And what was that?" he asked softly.

Julia tucked a curling lock of her hair behind her ear, a habit he suddenly realized he'd grown to enjoy watching. She smiled down into his face, and again his heart kicked against his ribs.

"You're my friend," she told him.

It seemed a simple statement, but Ryan could tell it held monumental importance to Julia.

"The hands-off rule is kind of silly if it's keeping us from our goal. Besides…" She looked away shyly for a moment, then her gaze was on him again, engrossing. "I feel safe with you. I *am* safe with you."

He twisted the cap off the bottle without taking his eyes from her beautiful face.

I've discovered something, too, Julia, he should have said. *And it's that, with me, you are anything but safe.*

Chapter Eight

"Mom?"

Julia looked up from the recipe book she was paging through. She really missed reading her romance novels. The colorful, glossy pictures of the pies and tarts were great, but they just couldn't compare to the emotional stories she was used to reading before bed.

"Come on in." She beckoned Kelly into her room with a smile, and patted a space beside her on the bed in a silent invitation to sit. "Are you okay?"

Kelly shrugged. "I guess." The mattress sagged as she eased onto it.

Julia felt a pang of guilt flash through her. She'd been busy the past couple of weeks, what with lunching with Ryan every day and then making up that time spent away from Gold Ribbon by working through dinner each evening. And he'd taken her out several times in the evening in an effort to put on a good show for Kelly. Spending time with her daughter had sort of fallen by the wayside.

"Could we talk?" Kelly asked.

The smile on her mouth widened and her heart warmed. "We sure can. What's up?"

Another shrug. "Nothin' in particular," she said, looking off at the far corner of the room.

Julia could clearly see her daughter had something worrisome on her mind. However, all she could do was wait until Kelly was ready to disclose whatever it was.

Finally, Kelly lifted her dark eyes. "You and Ryan have been seein' a lot of each other."

So, Julia thought, this had to do with Ryan. "Yes," she said, "we have."

A moment of silence followed. A moment during which Julia felt her daughter was sorting out her thoughts.

"Is your relationship getting, like, serious?"

Kelly's head tilted just a fraction when she spoke the last word. The concern shadowing her daughter's eyes confused Julia.

Steering the conversation into a slightly different direction, Julia said, "I thought this was what you wanted, Kelly. I'm dating. I'm having a good time. I'm not spending every waking minute working."

"I do want this for you," Kelly was quick to say. "I'm happy that you and Ryan are together." She paused, frowning. "At least, I think I am."

A crease bit into Julia's brow. "What do you mean?"

Kelly's shoulder hitched up. "I don't know. I can't help feeling a little...scared."

Pushing her fists against the mattress, Julia scooted to a more upright position and leaned against the headboard. "Honey," she said, astonished by her daughter's admission, "why on earth would you feel afraid of my relationship with Ryan?"

The forgotten cookbook was pushed to the side as Kelly curled up next to her mother, laying her head on the coverlet spread across Julia's lap.

"I don't know," Kelly whispered. "I do want you to be happy. I don't want you to think I'm being selfish."

Julia smoothed her fingertips over Kelly's dark, satiny hair. "I'm not going to think you're selfish, honey. Tell me what's troubling you."

Her knees drew up to a near fetal position and that told Julia just how distressed Kelly was feeling.

"I like Ryan," she began. "I like him a lot. It's just that…"

The child's prone position made her shrug difficult to maneuver and her shoulder gently collided with Julia's thigh.

"I don't want him—" Kelly's tone dropped to a mere whisper "—or anyone, to come between you and me."

Hearing Kelly's fear voiced in that little-girl-lost tone made Julia's heart ache with compassion. No one but a mother could possibly understand how a child could snip and snarl, complain and argue for days on end and then curl up in a tiny, vulnerable ball to confess her deepest dread to the one person with whom she'd been fighting so fiercely.

Julia closed her eyes, willing away the tears that splintered her sight. She had to be strong. To reassure her daughter that she'd always be loved.

Now would be the perfect time to tell Kelly the absolute truth. That she and Ryan had a bargain. A deal. A mutually beneficial arrangement. Telling her daughter that the relationship she and Ryan shared had nothing whatsoever to do with love or commitment or devotion would put the child's mind at ease, once and for all.

But *was* that the truth? She pressed her lips together,

the question humming in her head like a haunting tune that refused to go away.

Her afternoons and evenings with Ryan had been filled with friendly conversation and lots of flirtatious teasing. Something had happened between them since that kiss they had shared. The awkward wall she'd erected between them had been demolished, and now the thick atmosphere of attraction was free to surround them. Both of them enjoyed testing this new closeness, capering on this new playground they had created.

Julia had wished that some situation would arise where she would be forced to touch him, to kiss him. She prayed that Cherry would show up during one of their lunches. But the sultry redhead hadn't made a second visit to Ryan's office, and Julia had been left feeling frustrated.

And although it went against everything she'd ever wanted for herself, Julia had to admit that she had contemplated what it would be like to have Ryan in her life. For real.

She looked down at her daughter's dark head in her lap. Julia didn't want to lie to Kelly about where her future relationship with Ryan might be heading. But she *could* reassure her in a way only a mother could, and she could do it by telling Kelly the honest-to-goodness truth.

"Kelly," she said softly, "you don't ever have to worry about anyone coming between us." She slid her fingers over the child's soft cheek. "I love you. You're the most important part of my life. And no man—not Ryan, or anyone else—can ever change that."

Her entire body seemed to swell with love when Kelly snuggled closer and asked, "You really mean it?"

"With all my heart," she said without hesitation.

Kelly took a deep breath and exhaled slowly, and Julia could feel the contentment emanating off the child like a soft fragrance. This was what motherhood was all about, Julia thought. Loving unconditionally.

Yes, she made mistakes. She and Kelly fought at times like cats and dogs. But during quiet times like these, Julia knew the meaning of pure love. Being a mom brought perfect moments of serene gratification and deep, unequaled satisfaction. She wouldn't have missed this for the world.

"Mom," Kelly said.

"Hmm?" Julia felt wrapped in a warm blanket of tenderness.

"What's it feel like? To be kissed, I mean."

Every muscle in Julia's body tensed in a knee-jerk kind of fashion, and sensing her mother's anxiety, Kelly sat up.

Words tumbled from Julia's mouth before she took the time to think. "Why do you want to know that?" she asked. She was startled by the harsh tone of her voice, but was helpless to stop it.

"Sorry." Kelly's apology was mumbled and curt, and she was off the bed in an instant. "Forget it. Forget I asked." And she turned toward the door.

Julia's mind was racing. Her first impulse was to slam shut the door on this sexual discussion. To let her daughter go without another word. Kelly was too young to be asking such a question.

But, a tiny voice intoned from somewhere in the back of her brain, *isn't that just what your own father did to you? Didn't he cut off communication in the hopes of snuffing out your curiosity?*

That's exactly what he'd done, Julia sadly admitted.

And did his tactics work?

She nearly groaned, knowing her father's parenting tactics only heightened her teenage fascination, and the resulting situation nearly destroyed her whole life.

"Kelly, wait," she said. "Come back, honey. Let's talk."

Her daughter stood in the doorway, her expression dubious.

"I mean it," Julia assured her. "I want to talk. I want to answer your questions."

Kelly seemed tentative and unsure when she sat back down on the edge of the mattress, yet Julia couldn't help but notice the tiny spark of interest lighting the child's dark eyes.

Suddenly a thought occurred to her—if Kelly was asking what kissing was like, then it sounded like the child hadn't participated in the act. That relieved Julia's mind, especially after knowing how her daughter had slipped out of the house to go to the movies with that boy. But even though she was relieved, Julia also felt a tremendous wave of panic that had her scrambling to decide what to say. How much to disclose.

Simply answer her questions honestly, the parent in her silently advised. No more, no less.

"Okay," Julia whispered when it became evident that Kelly was growing impatient for her to begin. "What's it like to be kissed?" Absently, she reached up and touched her lips, remembering the feel of Ryan's mouth on hers.

"Well," she haltingly started, "kissing is kind of…warm, and cozy. Kissing is a soft and tender way of saying you care about someone. Someone who's special."

She couldn't help but keep her words elementary, her descriptions basic. Kelly was only fourteen years old.

The child didn't need to hear about the lava-like passion a kiss could invoke.

So often over the past two weeks Julia had relived the hot, delicious kiss she and Ryan had shared. The kiss had been spontaneous. An impulsive act caused by Cherry's rude statements.

But the kiss had taken place, Julia suddenly realized, because she cared about Ryan. And as the weeks wore on, she was finding she cared for him more and more. The feelings churning inside her were dangerous and frightening, but at the same time they were exciting.

"I know that kissing is an act of...of..." here Kelly stammered for a moment. "Devotion. But how does it *feel?*"

This was a monumental moment between mother and daughter, Julia knew. Kelly was making herself vulnerable, opening her heart and her emotions by asking these intimate questions. Julia wasn't so old that she forgot what a completely natural thing it was for a teenager to dream of her first kiss.

"It feels nice." Julia inhaled deeply. "Sharing a kiss makes you feel special. Warm. Close. It's...very nice."

A small sigh escaped Kelly. "I want to feel special."

Suppressing a smile, Julia told her, "You know, you already are special. You don't need to be kissed by a boy to—"

"Mo-ther." Kelly rolled her eyes and stretched the single word into two long syllables. "You know what I mean."

"I know exactly what you mean," she said. "I want you to realize that you should always think things through. Know why you're doing what you're doing. And don't do things for the wrong reasons. You don't need this boy's approval, and—"

"Thanks, Mom," Kelly cut her off, rising to a stand and then to the door in one swift motion. "Thanks for talking to me."

Too late, Julia realized she'd ruined their mother-daughter moment the instant she'd slipped into lecture mode. "Wait a minute—"

"I gotta go call Sheila." Suddenly she turned back to face her mother. "Oh, by the way," she said, her tone tingeing with rebellion, "*that boy* you keep referring to…his name is Tyler. And he isn't moving away anytime soon."

Julia relaxed against the headboard, closing her eyes and listening to the quiet. Why did she fall into that rut? she wondered. Why the lecture? Why the admonishing tone?

A heaving sigh passed her lips. Such behavior was simply a mother's curse, she guessed.

Ryan hung the telephone receiver onto its cradle on the wall and shook his head in wonder.

"I don't believe it," he said.

"What?" Charlotte asked. "Who was that on the phone?"

The delicious aroma of mushrooms sizzling in olive oil and garlic wafted in the air, but Ryan was barely aware of it.

"That was Cherry."

"Oh?" His cousin took a moment to note the amount of salt she'd just added to the recipe she was creating. Then she looked at him. "Was it good news? Or bad?"

"Ah," he said, stalling for time to sort through his confused emotions. "I'm not sure."

Charlotte set down her pencil. "What do you mean, Ryan?"

"I'm—" he shook his head "—not sure."

Seemingly without thought, she took hold of the frying pan handle, shook the contents, and with a flick of her wrist, deftly flipped the vegetables several times before returning them to the burner.

"Well, I'm sure of one thing," she said, grinning. "You're befuddled enough to be repeating yourself."

Ryan didn't comment on the teasing remark. Instead he said, "Cherry just gave me two addresses for apartments. She said I'd have to go on my own. That she didn't have time to go with me. And then she said the most extraordinary thing."

After a moment of silence, Charlotte's frustration got the best of her and had her asking, "What? What'd she say?"

He swallowed. "She said…she's got a date."

"Great!" His cousin's smile was huge. "Then it *is* good news."

It was good news, Ryan told himself. Wasn't it?

He let the idea sink in. If Cherry had a date, that meant she was moving to other hunting grounds. She was no longer drawing a bead on him in her quest for a husband. So, that was good news. Wasn't it?

This turn of events also meant that he and Julia would no longer need to play at dating one another. At least not because of Cherry. He could free Julia from his part of their bargain. So that, too, was good news. Wasn't it?

Yes, he thought. Both those things were very good news.

So why did he feel so…let down? Disappointed?

He'd enjoyed himself immensely since he'd made this arrangement with Julia. Maybe he'd even relished this time with her too much.

"Ryan?"

Jerking to attention, he blinked and focused on Charlotte. "I'm sorry. You said something?"

"Yeah." She chuckled. "I said this is great news."

He nodded, even though his neck muscles didn't seem to want to cooperate. "I guess it is."

"I'm sure Julia will be relieved."

She seemed not to notice his hesitation, and for that he was grateful. All of a sudden, breathing became difficult.

"You're right." Ryan spoke around the stress that choked him. "She'll be glad to find out we don't have to put on this romantic act anymore."

Charlotte sprinkled some fragrant, freshly chopped herb into the pan. She stirred the mushrooms and then set down the spatula. "Ryan," she said, "why does it seem that you're not feeling so good about this good news?"

Damn, Ryan thought, she had noticed his uncertainty.

Charlotte rested her fist on her hip. "Okay, what gives?"

"I'm not sure."

His cousin laughed, and he wished like hell he could laugh with her. But he couldn't. Neither could he quite figure out what the heck was the matter with him.

He *did* want Cherry to move on. He *did* want her to set her romantic sights on someone else. That was why he'd gotten caught up in this harebrained scheme with Julia to begin with.

It was his relationship with Julia that had his emotions all twisted up in knots.

"What are you thinking about?" Charlotte asked.

With a shrug, he answered simply, "Julia." He heaved a sigh. "I didn't want to care about her. Didn't want my feelings to get personal." He combed his fingers through his hair. "I didn't plan on getting close to her."

"But you have."

It took him a moment to answer. "I'm not sure."

She narrowed her eyes at him, looking for the truth.

His chuckle didn't have a bit of humor in it. "Yeah," he said, "I guess I have gotten close to her." He leaned his hip against the kitchen counter and crossed his arms over his chest. "But, Charlotte, you know it's useless. Couples don't have a chance these days. They split up right and left. Look at my parents, look at you. Hell, look at Cherry."

"Hey," Charlotte warned, "don't be basing any kind of romantic relationship on Cherry's batting average. She gives couples everywhere a bad reputation."

Ryan had to laugh at his cousin's acute observation. "You're right," he said. Then a serious expression took over his features. "Then let's talk about you. Would you have married Harry if you knew what was going to happen to your marriage?"

She thought a long moment before she answered. Finally she said, "You want the truth? I think I would have. We shared enough good times that I'd have said those vows all over again..." she twisted her lips up at one corner. "Even if I knew in the end he was going to be a slimeball."

Charlotte took the sauté pan off the heat. "Ryan, you can't go through your life all alone just because you *think* you know what the future's going to bring."

"But statistically—"

"Forget statistics," she said. "If you have feelings for Julia, you should tell her."

"Why?" he asked. "She's just as much against relationships as I am.'' Before his cousin could comment he said, ''Do you have any idea why?''

Charlotte turned the steaming mushrooms onto a platter and sprinkled them with grated pecorino cheese and some toasted breadcrumbs. ''I don't,'' she admitted. ''Julia's never been very open about her past. And I've never been one to pry.''

She speared a glistening mushroom with a fork and held it to his lips, offering it to him to taste. ''But if you've fallen in love—''

''*Love?*'' Ryan nearly choked as he swallowed, oblivious to the rich, earthy flavors on his tongue. ''Who said anything about love?''

In asking the question, he realized that he was implying that he *didn't* have deep and special feelings for Julia, and even though he hated to admit it, he knew that was a lie. He may not be able to figure out exactly what those feelings were or how deep they went, but he knew he was feeling them just the same.

''You're right,'' Charlotte muttered. ''You and Julia are both just as stubborn when it comes to matters of the heart.''

After a moment, she asked, ''So…what do you think?''

Ryan pursed his lips, inhaling deeply. ''I think you're right. I need to tell Julia how I feel. I want to ask why she feels the way she does about relationships.'' He nodded. ''Yeah, Julia and I need to talk.''

An ironic smile tweaked Charlotte's mouth. ''I'm happy you've come to that conclusion,'' she said. ''But I was asking what you think of my mushroom dish.''

''Oh.'' He darted a glance down at the platter and then back up to Charlotte's face. ''It's good. Delicious, actually.'' He lifted his hand and worried his earlobe between his fingers. "But I still think Julia and I need to talk. I really want to find out why she's got this hang-up about men."

Julia pulled open the front door and offered Ryan a welcoming smile.

"Hi," he said, and he held out a small bouquet of cut daisies.

Her smile widened. "They're beautiful. Thanks." She took a backward step so he could come inside.

She felt her mouth twisting involuntarily, and her chest tightened with anxiety as she said, "We don't have to do this tonight. I mean, you don't have to stay if you have something else you'd rather do. You see, Kelly's not here. She went out with her best friend. Sheila's mom is taking the girls to a movie. And then out for ice cream."

There was a definite nervous quality to her short, spurting sentences.

"Kelly won't be home until late," she continued. "She won't even know that you were here. I mean, ah, unless I tell her. And of course I mean to. But you don't have to stay." She lifted one shoulder. "Faking a date tonight would be kind of silly. Seeing as how Kelly's not here to see us together."

His deep blue eyes softened, and his smile melted away all the nervous anxiety that had her muscles clenched tight.

"I'd like to stay," he told her. "That is, if you don't mind? I'd like to talk to you."

Julia felt a wave of joy, warm and sunny, wash over her whole body. She'd hoped he would stay even though Kelly was not home. She'd prayed that he'd want to spend time with her even though it wasn't necessary that he do so. Hearing him actually voice the words gave her a great deal of pleasure.

"Great," she said. "I've made a strawberry tart, and there's a fresh pot of coffee waiting for us."

Soon they were seated in the living room, chuckling and chatting about what had happened to each of them over the course of the day. He told her about Charlotte's scrumptious new mushroom recipe, and she told him about the closeness she'd shared with Kelly. Of course Julia couldn't bring herself to reveal the sexual nature of her talk with her daughter, or the curt manner in which the conversation had ended.

"But for the most part," she said, "things are okay between me and Kelly." Then she grinned and added, "For the moment, anyway."

Julia was amazed by the attention Ryan focused on her, as if he really wanted to hear all about the mundane happenings in her life. And she didn't miss the fact that, when he talked, she found herself eager for his words. It was almost as if the two of them were an old, married couple. Comfortable with each other. Anxious to listen to what the other had to say.

However, the underlying current of attraction that pulsed between them with a steady beat kept Julia from becoming *too* comfortable.

"Would you like more coffee?" she asked.

"No, thanks." He set his empty cup onto its saucer on the end table. "You know—" his blue gaze turned serious "—I've really enjoyed spending this time with you."

She smiled. His words seemed so sincere and her heart expanded in her chest. She, too, liked being with him, and she found herself wondering just what it would be like to spend every single evening of her life with this man. Would her attraction for him wane? She doubted it. Would the friendly camaraderie they shared ever fade? Again, she doubted that it would.

She knew she distrusted men. Knew that it was that distrust that had kept her all alone all these years. But if there was ever a man she felt she might gift with her trust…that man would be Ryan.

Spontaneously, she reached out and touched his knee, hoping the gesture would silently communicate her heartfelt thoughts. Proclaim the feelings she wasn't yet able to actually voice.

Julia knew she was going to have to find the strength to overcome her distrust. She was going to have to somehow garner the strength it would take to conquer this blinding fear of hers so she could tell Ryan how she felt about him.

He reached out and took her hand, his strong fingers sliding over hers. "I have some good news," he said quietly.

"I love hearing good news." She sat there, basking in the warmth of his touch.

One corner of his mouth tipped up in a charming grin that squeezed at Julia's heart. She loved this warm fuzziness enveloping her.

"Cherry's given up on me," he said. "We don't have to play this dating game anymore."

She grew stone-still. She hadn't been ready for this. Hadn't expected this turn of events. The shock of what she heard seemed to quick-freeze her insides into a solid block of ice. She was so dumbfounded by what he'd said that she felt totally paralyzed. Her smile never faltered, though, her upturned mouth frigid and numb.

"You've been great through this whole mess," Ryan said.

Rejection.

The cruel word reverberated through her head as if it had been shouted in a large, cold tomb.

The overwhelming urge to cry enveloped her like a soupy, sweltering fog. But her eyes remained bone dry, the tears being shed only by the silent, forlorn child in her head, in her heart.

Her relationship with Ryan was over. He'd used past tense verbs just seconds ago when referring to the enjoyment he'd felt during the time they'd spent together. Why hadn't she noticed that? Why hadn't it registered in her brain?

Instead, she'd allowed herself to become all tangled up in her feelings for him. She shivered when she thought of how desperately she'd wanted to tell him of those feelings. But her strong, self-preserving instinct had silenced her. That instinct had saved her from making a complete and utter fool of herself.

"Julia?"

He squeezed her fingers, the pressure reminding her that he still held her hand, that a stupid smile was still plastered to her face.

Rejection.

The harsh, rusty word nearly made her wince with physical pain.

She straightened her spine, pulling her hand from his. Setting down her coffee cup, she took a deep breath to try to calm the chaos reigning in her head, but it was an impossible task.

She'd thought Ryan was different. She'd thought he was a man who could be trusted.

"Isn't that great?" he asked.

Julia nodded, still unable to coax words from her lips. How could he expect her to act cordial? she wondered. How could he dump this on her, reject her like this, and expect her to remain gracious and friendly?

Then she averted her gaze as she was struck with a revelation. She, not Ryan, was the one who had gotten caught up in all these intimate emotions. She was the one who had allowed herself to react to, to fantasize about, this heated attraction she felt for him. How could she blame him for these awful feelings swirling and tumbling inside her when he was simply sticking to the terms of their deal?

Finally, she forced herself to speak.

"I, ah, I'm happy, Ryan," she said, her voice tight, corroded by the bitterness threatening to choke her. "Really. I am. I'm glad that you were able to solve your problem with Cherry and…and not damage your friendship with her father."

He looked so relieved. Relieved to have that redheaded vixen out of his life. Relieved that he no longer had to act out a love relationship with Julia that didn't exist.

She felt so humiliated that she'd put herself in the position to be hurt. Set herself up. Again. After all the years of promising herself she'd never let history be repeated.

Rejection.

"I can't tell you how happy I was to get Cherry's call," Ryan said. "It's over. And I'm really pleased that it is." Then he reached out and touched her lightly on the knee. "But I want you to know that I'll keep up my end of our bargain. For Kelly's sake, I mean. For as long as you need me to—"

"I don't." She cut him off sharply, his bewildered frown barely registering in the frenzy of her thoughts.

The need to break free of this bargain of theirs nearly choked her with its intensity.

Brushing his hand from her leg, she tightened her hands into fists of steel and stood all in one brusque motion. The force was enough to have her bumping into the coffee table, rattling her cup in its saucer.

"I don't *need* you," she said, her eyes narrowing. "I don't *need* any man." Her chest was rising and falling, rising and falling, at an alarming rate. "I don't need your help with Kelly. I can raise my daughter all on my own. I've been doing it for years. I'm the only constant thing in that child's life. I've worked hard to see she's had a steady source of unconditional love. You think I'd let some man into our lives to ruin that?"

Chapter Nine

She expected him to be furious. She expected him to be insulted. She expected—no, she *wanted* him to become so infuriated by what she'd said that he stomp out of her house. Out of her life. Forever.

She hadn't expected the utterly calm cloak he slipped into. Or the gentle concern that softened his deep blue eyes.

"Sit down, Julia."

His suggestion was warm and feathery as worn velvet, and Julia found herself wanting desperately to obey. But there was all manner of dark and chilling emotions that kept her knees locked tight, emotions she didn't dare examine too closely at the moment.

"Please," he said, and he reached out to her, his fingertips skimming across her forearm.

His touch was like liquid heat seeping into her bones, thawing her frozen muscles, and she eased her body down onto the edge of the couch. She felt strangely detached from the situation as strong and fearful feelings battled in her head with softer urges that couldn't quite be identified but were instinctively unwanted. Yet as withdrawn as she felt, she was still intrinsically aware of him, of his body movements, his facial expression.

"I have this feeling," Ryan began, "that it's not me you're angry with. That it's someone else. Someone who hurt you in some way."

Why didn't he just leave? her brain screamed. *Don't you let him pry into your past! Don't you dare let him in!*

"You're way out of line here," she said.

He ignored the warning. "You said a moment ago that you didn't need my help with Kelly. We both know that's not true." His tone was kindhearted. "If you didn't need me, then why did we enter into this bargain?"

She pressed her lips together until they felt hard and strained. She owed him no explanation and was damned determined not to offer one.

"You needed me," he said. "Just like I needed you."

Don't admit anything, her self-preserving instinct demanded.

"I observed all the rules, Julia. Right down the line." His blue gaze intensified. "*Your* rules," he reminded her. "When you said no physical touching, no handholding, no kissing, I agreed." He inhaled deeply. "And I agreed because, well, because I knew you had a...problem."

She clicked her tongue in disgust even while, inside, she was shocked and surprised by his awareness.

"I have no problem," she said, and she hated the fact that she was unable to look him directly in the eye.

He only gazed at her for one silent moment.

"You might not want to admit it to me," he said.

"But you know I'm right, Julia. You know what I'm saying is the truth."

It was then that he pulled his hand from her forearm, and the spot on her skin felt suddenly chilled.

"I was careful to maintain a distance in our relationship from the very beginning," he said, "even though there were times I didn't want to. And I maintained that distance because I sensed your…problem."

His hesitation irked the devil out of her. What did he think? That she was some wounded animal? "I don't have a problem," she snapped.

She was vaguely aware that he'd revealed something of extreme importance, something she'd missed, but the fact that he kept insisting she suffered from some difficulty angered her. She would *not* let him into her head. Into her past. That place was just too painful to visit.

Again he ignored her angry statement.

"I thought, with all that we've shared with one another, that you had come to see me as your friend," he told her. "Someone who cares about you. I don't know who hurt you. I don't know if it was a month ago or ten years ago, but I do want to tell you that I'm ready to listen, whenever you're ready to talk."

There they were again, Julia realized, surging up inside her. Those soft, unidentified urges that battled so fiercely with the bitterness and anger roiling in her gut.

Ryan *had* followed all the rules, a tiny part of her brain admitted. He'd done everything she'd asked, and he'd requested nothing from her that she hadn't been willing to give.

He cares about you. The four words whispered through her head. He said so. And he means it. Doesn't he?

"I can't." Her lips nearly trembled and she clamped

her hand over them. "I can't talk about it. Not to you. Not to anyone."

It was then that she finally put a name to the warm and fuzzy impulses that warred inside her.

Trust. And *surrender.*

Julia knew she could do neither of those things. In fact, she'd given up on them years ago. They caused too much heartache, too much suffering.

"Sure you can, Julia."

His voice was sweet and enticing, as tempting as the taste of heated honey.

"Whatever it is," he said to her, "you can't keep it bottled up inside you forever. It isn't good. It isn't healthy." After a moment, he added, "It isn't fair. To you or the people who care about you."

"I'm afraid."

Hearing Julia admit to her fear, Ryan knew without a doubt she was about to confide in him when she probably hadn't ever confided in anyone before. His heart swelled with heated emotion, and a gentle compassion.

Then he felt a fear of his own—the fear of intimacy—spark to life, hot and sulfurous, like the lighting of a match. He must be crazy to be opening himself up like this. In admitting his concern for Julia, he was changing their relationship. Pulling her closer to him. And that only made him vulnerable to being hurt.

But he was being honest when he'd told her he cared. He really did. If voicing that worry and concern left him susceptible to a little pain, he was ready and willing. So, he snuffed out the fear. He had to remain strong. Julia needed him. And he intended to be here for her.

"Don't be afraid," he told her.

He wrapped his arms around her body and pulled her

to him until her back was snuggled against his chest. He felt the dread emanating off her, and he knew the telling would be easier if she wasn't looking him in the face.

She was quiet for a long time. But he could be patient.

"It was…" she began, but then faltered to a stop. "It was a long time ago."

"How long?" he softly prompted.

Her inhalation was shaky. "Before Kelly was born."

Ryan frowned. She'd lived with this pain for so many years.

Again there was a moment of silence, and he found himself wondering what man in Julia's life had hurt her. Kelly's father? Her own father?

Mentally, he calculated the years. Kelly was fourteen. Before that, Julia would have been in her late teens. She simply hadn't been old enough to have had too many experiences with men.

"My mother died when I was just a baby," Julia revealed. "My father raised me on his own. He was—"

She paused for a nervous swallow.

"Very strict. Overly protective of me. I wasn't allowed to date. Wasn't even allowed to have friends of the opposite sex."

Ryan couldn't help but notice how her trouble with Kelly paralleled her own dilemma when she'd been a teen. He must have tensed, must have given his thoughts away in some manner, because Julia twisted around and looked him in the eyes.

"I know what you're thinking," she said defensively. "That I'm perpetuating the problem. That I'm doing to Kelly the same thing my father did to me. But I'm not. Kelly is fourteen years old, Ryan. *Fourteen.* She's not ready to be making decisions that will affect the rest of her life."

He actually felt her body growing more and more agitated. Her eyes were rounded, her shoulders tense.

"Relax," he told her. "I'm not making any judgments here. Besides, we weren't talking about Kelly. We were talking about you."

There would be plenty of time to talk about the here and now, he thought. At this moment, the past needed to be dealt with.

"But I need you to understand." Her midnight gaze implored him. "There *is* a difference. I was seventeen. Nearly an adult. And I wasn't allowed to talk to boys on the phone. I wasn't allowed to have them over to my house. It was like something out of the Middle Ages. God forbid I should even suggest going out on a date. My father would have had a heart attack—"

She started in his arms and the sharp movement seemed to choke off her words.

"What is it?" he asked, pulling her securely against his chest. "What are you thinking?"

"He did have a heart attack." The words escaped her in a painful whisper. "No, not a heart attack," she corrected. "A stroke. I caused my father to have a stroke."

His heart nearly split in two at the agony she expressed. "Now, Julia—"

"I *did,* I'm telling you." Unwittingly she reached up and curled her fingers over his forearm. "I was a horrible daughter. I sneaked out of the house. Many times. I sneaked out to be with a boy. A boy who said he loved me."

Her hold on him tightened. "I was young. And I was stupid. Because I believed in that love."

Then she turned in his embrace until she was once again pressed against his chest and she whispered, "I got myself pregnant."

"Oh, Julia. Sweet Julia." Ryan leaned his cheek gently against the side of her head, hoping to give her comfort, even though he knew nothing he could say or do right now would soften the pain she was feeling in reliving these memories.

"The worst night of my life was when I told Kelly's father we were having a baby...."

Ryan felt a fat tear drip onto his hand and knew she'd begun to cry. All he could do was hold her tight. Offer what comfort he could.

"He laughed in my face," she went on. "Said he didn't want anything to do with me. Said he didn't want anything to do with any baby. He said he refused to allow me to ruin his life."

Her breath caught in her throat and her next words came out sounding gritty as finely crushed stone.

"He advised me to get an abortion. And if I told anyone he was the father of our baby that he'd—" A sob wrenched her. "He said he'd deny having slept with me."

The anguish made her shoulders shake, her tears flow.

"Julia," Ryan crooned, "that boy was young. He was immature. He had no idea what he was saying. No idea what he was doing. To you. To Kelly. Or to himself."

"He was older than I was." She shot the statement at him in a burst of anger. "He'd already graduated high school. He had a job and everything. He'd said he loved me. I thought sure he'd love our child. But he'd only been using me, Ryan." Her tone lowered. "He'd only been using me."

Her agony made Ryan's anger burn. He clenched his teeth, his jaw brushing against her silky hair. "He was a dirty, stinking rat. That's what he was." But she didn't seem to hear him.

"The worst part came when I got home that night," Julia said. "My father caught me coming in my bedroom window."

Lord, Ryan thought, no wonder Julia had been so distressed by Kelly's behavior.

"We got into a fight, Ryan. An awful fight. I didn't tell him about the baby. Not then. I didn't get the chance. He…he became confused suddenly. Unable to speak. And I ended up having to call for help."

"Julia," Ryan said, hugging her to him. "I'm so sorry."

"I went to visit him in the hospital every day. Scared to death, knowing that I'd have to tell him about the baby growing inside me. The baby I was going to have to raise all on my own."

An icy shiver coursed through her, strong enough that he felt it, and then she trembled as if she were cold.

"When he was finally well enough, I broke the news to him."

Fresh tears fell on his skin.

"He was so hostile," she said. "He ordered me to put the baby up for adoption. He said he just wasn't up to raising another child."

Her grasp on his forearm tightened and she seemed to be holding on for dear life.

"I just couldn't do that." The words were shaky. "I just couldn't give my baby away."

"Of course you couldn't," he whispered.

After a brief pause, she continued with her story. "I graduated that June. Pregnant. Friendless. Ostracized. And the day after graduation—" she took a deep breath "—I ran away. I ran far away. I couldn't let my father take away my child."

"How did you survive?" The question slipped from

his lips, so desperate was he to know. "What did you do? Who did you go to for help?"

He tried to imagine how alone and frightened Julia must have felt as a seventeen-year-old runaway, and the effort alone left him feeling bleak and helpless. She must have been so scared.

But at the same time, he had to admire her strength of will. Her maternal instinct had been powerful, even at that young age.

"A truck driver picked me up along I-95."

The words came out sounding dreamy, as if she were reliving the memory rather than just relating it.

"He was really nice," she said.

Ryan couldn't see her face, but he felt her body relax, sensed the sad smile that took over her expression.

"He fed me. I'd never been so hungry in my life. He just sat there watching me eat. And when I finished my meal, he gave me his. He left the table. I'd thought he'd gone to use the rest room, but when he came back, he handed me a telephone number."

Sitting there with her cradled in his arms, Ryan didn't dare move a muscle for fear of jolting her out of this daydreamy state.

"The Sisters took me in. They fed me, along with two other teenage runaways. They didn't ask any questions about where I'd come from. I was terribly grateful for that. After Kelly was born, the Sisters asked me what I wanted to do. They said they could contact a state agency and find a good home for Kelly, but I was adamant that I meant to raise my daughter. The Sisters didn't abandon me. They helped me find a job. Did everything they could to get me on my feet. I owe them a lot."

A light puff of warm air grazed across his skin as Julia sighed.

"I send the Sisters a donation every year, but I stopped going back to visit. I didn't want Kelly to know about the awful circumstances surrounding her birth. Didn't want her to know how the two of us had been rejected by the very people who were supposed to love us." She reached up and passed her hand across her forehead. "Who am I kidding? I stopped going back for me. I needed to put it behind me. I needed to forget."

She squirmed out of his embrace and twisted her body until she was facing him. The haunted look in her black-as-night gaze nearly brought tears to his eyes.

"But I haven't forgotten, Ryan. I haven't forgotten." She blinked, and a single tear strolled slowly down her cheek. "And I never will."

Reaching out, Ryan cupped her jaw in his palm. He didn't touch the tear. Didn't dare wipe it away. The tears she was crying had been a long time in coming. They needed to be shed. This pain needed to be felt.

"That's okay, Julia," he said softly. "Maybe you weren't meant to forget. Everything you went through is a part of who you are. Your past has helped to mold you. It's made you a good mother for Kelly. Deeply loving. Deeply caring. The pain you've suffered has forced you to become an incredibly strong woman. A woman Kelly can depend on. Look up to."

"You really think so?"

Her sexy eyes lit with a tiny ray of hope, and the gratitude he read on her beautiful face made his throat swell shut. Because he could get no words out, he simply nodded.

Pausing a moment, he forced himself to relax. He had so much more he wanted to say to this wonderful woman who looked at him with her dark, sad eyes. There was so much more she needed to hear.

"If you hadn't defied your father," he said. "If you hadn't sneaked out to meet with your boyfriend, or fallen in love and given yourself to him, if you had listened to what Kelly's father wanted you to do about the pregnancy, or to what your own father wanted you to do…" He hesitated for effect. "If you hadn't run away from home, if you hadn't gone through all that you did, then you wouldn't have Kelly. Can you image your life without your daughter?"

He watched her face fall as he listed all the terrible events of her life. Now he wanted desperately to take away her pain, kiss away her tears, stroke away all her bad memories. And without any other thought in his head, he let his fingers slide along her jaw, under her hair, to curl around the creamy silken skin of her nape.

She studied his face, his question churning up her thoughts, but she didn't have too much time to ponder it before her heart began to patter swiftly against her ribs.

Ryan was going to kiss her. She sensed it, saw it, and the realization made her feel like a tiny wild bird on the verge of being tamed, wanting desperately to fly away to safety yet also frantic to stay perched right where she was.

Trust. Surrender.

The words reverberated into her thoughts like a warm, heady elixir.

And almost as if he'd read her mind, he whispered, "Trust me, Julia. Please."

He inched closer, pulling her toward him at the same time until they met halfway. When they were but a breath apart, he paused to gaze deeply into her eyes. That's when she felt it. A connection. An intrinsic attachment that was a mixture of pure physical attraction and something deeper. Something much more emotional. Something she'd never felt before.

What she'd thought was love at the young age of seventeen didn't begin to compare with this in any way, shape or form. The feeling she'd shared with Kelly's father had been strong, yes. But it had been based totally on the physical, as teenage hormonal relationships are doomed to be. Shallow and frivolous in contrast to this soul-felt, visceral tenderness.

When he pressed his lips to hers, she closed her eyes and allowed herself to become lost in the scent of him, the feel of him, the taste of him. She'd denied herself this kind of physical pleasure for so long. So very long.

He tasted of warm, rich coffee with just a hint of sweet strawberries, and she suddenly realized he must be tasting the same flavors on her lips. His tongue brushed across her delicate skin and she felt a glorious shiver resonate through her body.

Opening her mouth to him, she nearly sighed and relaxed against his chest. Their tongues met, touching tentatively and then engaging in a slow, erotic ritual that was as old as time itself.

One of his hands was resting on the back of her neck, the other on her shoulder. He slid his fingers into her hair, over her scalp, and the feel of his touch was so alien, so wonderful, that her breath left her in a rush.

"Are you okay?" he asked, his mouth still close against hers.

Words failed her, so in answer, she deepened the kiss further, smoothing her flattened palms over the soft fabric of his shirt. His pectoral muscles were firm and warm, his heartbeat pounded against her hand, and she couldn't deny the delight she felt knowing she caused this reaction in him.

His lips left her mouth, and he trailed fiery little kisses all along her jaw. She felt his hot tongue as he tasted her earlobe. When he gently nipped at her neck, an involuntary gasp leaped from her throat.

He said her name, his voice as hot and passionate as his kiss. The sound of his breathing, so close to her ear, started concentric quivery waves radiating through all the muscles in her body.

She felt his touch, gossamer, almost ethereal, in what seemed like several places at once. Her neck. Her shoulder. Her arm. Her waist.

Heat rolled and boiled in the very center of her. In the very deepest part of her feminine being. And when his palm slid up to cup her breast, it was as though he'd increased the flame beneath an already simmering pressure cooker.

It was her turn now to murmur his name, the sound of it swollen with desire as it tumbled from her mouth. She felt out of control. Amazingly, astoundingly, out of control.

In the blink of an eye, the catch of a breath, the buttons of her blouse were unfastened. He slipped the fabric from her shoulders and tossed it aside.

Completely caught up in this passionate frenzy, she tugged at the front of his shirt, struggled with the buttons, until they were undone. In less than an instant, his shirt was lying in a crumpled heap on the floor. His skin was smooth and hot and taut, his muscles firm and well-defined.

Even as she shifted her position, planting her knees in the center of the couch cushion, he kissed her. Her shoulder, and forearm, and chest, his lips as hot as blue flame.

With one small snap, he unfastened the plastic clasp nestled in her cleavage and her bra came free, the straps sliding over her shoulders and down her upper arms. He cupped her breasts in his hands, smoothing them, kneading them, until she thought sure she'd go mad with wanting. A dark, moist pulse beat deep within her, a pulse that grew needier by the moment.

She heard their breathing, ragged and rough, and she weaved her fingers wantonly into his hair, pulling his face closer, ever closer to her. Pressing her cheek against the top of his tawny head, she closed her eyes and savored the feel of his lips on her skin. He kissed her mounded breasts, his fingertips stroking their sensitive undersides like flames of silken fire.

Her mind felt as if it were in utter chaos, her logic, swept completely away by this tumbling tempest. And her emotions... The feelings churning through her were clamorous, raging, turbulent. She might be unable to name them, but she was thoroughly enjoying each and every one. This riotous confusion was exciting. Thrilling to the very marrow of her bones.

She wanted Ryan to take her upstairs where they could be comfortable. She wanted him to strip her naked. To tumble onto the bed with her. To make hot, passionate love to her.

Lifting her head, she opened her eyes, intending to tug him up the stairs to her room.

But then she saw it, and the suggestion she was about to make froze in her throat.

Kelly. Her smiling face shone out at Julia from the school picture that sat on the desk in its carved wooden frame.

Julia felt as if she'd suddenly run headlong into a solid brick wall. Desire still pumped thickly through her veins, but the cold hand of logic seemed to grab her around the neck, squeezing common sense back into her lust-fogged brain.

"Ryan," she murmured. Then she inhaled deeply in an effort to still the pounding of her heart, the pulsing of the tremendous need buried inside her.

"Please." Her voice sounded frail and feathery, almost desperate. But he continued his passionate assault, seeming to take what she said as an urging forward rather than a request for him to stop. And to tell the honest truth, she wasn't really absolutely certain she wanted him to stop, or go on and on and on....

But again, the cold claws of logic raked across her thoughts, bringing with it icy questions. What was she doing? How had she allowed herself to surrender to this man? To this extent? How could she have contemplated taking him upstairs into her bed?

What had he done to earn her trust? she frantically wondered. Did he deserve her faith—as shaky as it was—simply because he'd asked her to trust him?

She'd thought she'd felt a connection with him. But could she trust her judgment? Could she really believe he felt the same emotional alliance she had?

Something was missing. Something vital. Her thoughts were short-circuiting to the point that she couldn't say what that something was exactly. But whatever it was, its absence relegated what was happening here to the lowest form of physicalness between a man and a woman. The idea made Julia literally shudder, and suddenly she felt...naked. Exposed.

Planting her hands firmly on his shoulders, she pushed

until several inches of dense, sultry air was between them.

He looked up at her, desire burning in his sapphire eyes. His strong hands moved outward, gripping her arms, and she knew he meant to pull her to him. If he did, Julia felt she would easily become once again caught up in the sweltering mood.

"Wait." This time the word came out sounding determined, resolute, and she was relieved.

His gaze lit with confusion and a large measure of frustration, and Julia felt guilt slice through her, sharp as a shard of glass. She shouldn't have let this happen, she thought. She shouldn't have become so lost in her desire for him.

"I can't do this," she told him. That frantic, desperate quality was back in her voice and she despised that. "You s-see," she stammered. "Kelly might…I just shouldn't…I—"

"You said Kelly was gone for the evening."

The disappointment she read on his face twisted the knife of guilt that was already imbedded up to the hilt in her chest.

"She is," Julia admitted. "Um, what I meant to say was—please try to understand this, Ryan—I can't do this. I can't participate in…in meaningless sex just because it feels good when I'm trying desperately to keep my daughter from doing that very thing. I have to practice what I preach. It's my responsibility to Kelly."

He didn't respond for a moment, but then he muttered, "Meaningless sex."

Julia thought he might have uttered the phrase as a question, but didn't take the time to ponder his implication. She was too lost in the guilt she was feeling. In the horror of realizing just how far she'd almost gone with Ryan. Just how much of herself she'd nearly given to him.

She sat back on her heels, searching with both her eyes and her hands for her blouse. The urge to cover herself was overwhelming, and she knew suddenly how insecure and vulnerable Eve must have felt the moment she'd been gifted with the knowledge of her physical body.

"Wait," Ryan said, reaching out to take hold of her arm.

Julia's eyes widened, not with alarm or fear, but with sudden recognition. He was angry. The emotion showed clearly in his gaze, in his taut jaw, in the defined muscles of his bare shoulders and chest. She found his expression accusatory and she simply had to look away.

Her fingers stilled a scant inch from where her blouse lay on the couch cushion, because as stark naked as she felt, the magnetic pull of his eyes was stronger. Instinctively, she covered her breasts with her arms as best she could and lifted her gaze to his.

"There is a huge difference," he said, "between what you're trying to keep Kelly innocent of and what is happening here. Between us. There's a distinction between kids experimenting with sex in the back seat of some car and two consenting adults..."

He seemed flustered for a moment, as if he was trying to come up with the perfect definition.

"Enjoying one another's company."

A black bolt of pure fury flashed through her. "Is that what we're doing?" she asked, snatching up her blouse and fumbling to turn the sleeves right side out. "Right is right and wrong is wrong, Ryan. And it's wrong to have sex simply because *it feels good.*" She put ugly emphasis on the words as she stuffed her arm into one blouse sleeve. "How am I supposed to make Kelly understand that there are rules to follow—rules meant to keep her safe—if I'm not willing to follow the rules myself?"

His jaw tensed, and she knew his anger was nothing more than pure sexual frustration. Well, he'd have to get over it. What? Did he think she was some ice maiden who wasn't feeling the effects of their sizzling encounter?

"Where I come from," he said, his voice seething, "there are different rules for kids and adults."

She stood up, shoving her other arm into the blouse and hearing the fabric strain as she forced herself into the garment.

"I think you should go, Ryan," she told him. "And I also think we should end our deal. Right here. Right now. I just can't see you anymore."

Julia felt as if she were drowning. She hadn't realized she was going to say those words. Her body trembled, and tears prickled painfully at the backs of her eyelids.

She couldn't let him see her cry. She couldn't. That would be the ultimate humiliation.

Pressing her hand against her mouth, she stifled the stormy emotions simmering just below the surface. She turned around sharply and ran away from him, out of the living room, down the hall and up the stairs, not stopping until she'd reached the safety and seclusion of her bedroom.

Only then, with her body flung across the bed, did she allow her tears to fall.

Chapter Ten

It simply *had* to be done. It would be a terrible and painful chore, one that Julia had spent the past three days worrying over and planning. But she saw no other way.

All the pieces of the puzzle had finally fit together as she'd laid on her bed crying, immediately after she'd run from Ryan.

The mere thought of him brought a tidal wave of emotion washing over her, painful emotion she'd tried hard these past few days to hide from. She'd worked like a demon was after her. She'd cooked new recipes until her arms were stiff and sore from stirring and kneading. She'd reorganized the business files of Gold Ribbon. Even the advertising mailing list had been updated. A tedious task she'd never seemed to have time to complete.

Reverting back to her workaholic behavior had kept her sane, had kept her thoughts off the gorgeous, golden-haired man who had captured her heart, who had nearly captured her body, as well.

Julia had kept her physical self safe from Ryan, but she hadn't been so lucky with her soul. She couldn't help feeling that he'd snatched it right out of her. That he'd captured the very essence of her, imprisoned it in the palm of his hand, and he didn't even know it.

The first time after the sexual ''incident'' that she'd gone to Charlotte's, Julia had steeled herself, fully expecting to see Ryan. However, she hadn't. She'd learned from Charlotte that he'd found an apartment and was busy overseeing the moving of his furniture that had been in storage in Dover. Charlotte had also told her that he'd hired a secretary, that he'd taken on so many new clients that he was considering hiring a legal assistant.

She was happy for Ryan. She held no animosity toward him. She knew it was she who had allowed her emotions to get tangled up in their bargain. And it was she who would have to pay the price. To suffer the feelings of loss and betrayal. Not that she'd felt betrayed by Ryan. No. It was her own heart that had betrayed her.

Ryan had simply been a man. A man who had only taken what she had been offering. There was no law against that, and heaven knew that very same thing had happened to her in the distant past.

Just as Ryan was unaware that he'd captivated and mesmerized her, he probably didn't realize that he was the one who had provided all the pieces to Julia's puzzle. The one that had fallen into place that terrible night. The puzzle that had made it possible for her to see what was missing in her mother-daughter relationship. She knew now, thanks to Ryan, why she and Kelly were constantly at odds over this dating business.

She'd cried for a long time after she'd heard Ryan close the front door of her home. She'd cried for herself; for the teenager who had been rejected by the boy she loved; for the daughter who felt she had no other alternative than to run away from home; for the woman who had made the terrible mistake of falling in love with a man who only wanted to "enjoy" her physically. She'd wept until she'd felt utterly spent and she'd laid there thinking about her past, about all the things she'd told Ryan.

The memories Julia had of her father were filled with sternness…an uncompromising and rigid authoritarianism that left her feeling completely controlled. And she remembered hating her life, and her father. Is that what she wanted for Kelly?

That's when the puzzle began fitting together. That's when the idea of talking to Kelly had been born. That's also when Julia knew she'd have to go through the terrible chore of telling her daughter about her own past. There was no other way to make Kelly really understand Julia's fear. No other way to relate the loneliness and rejection of her own teenage experience.

When Kelly had been just a toddler, Julia had taught her to stay away from the stove—not simply because mommy said no, but because she'd taken the time to explain how hot pots and pans could burn. Likewise, when Julia had taught Kelly how to cross the street, she'd explained why looking both ways would keep her safe. Kelly had learned all her childhood lessons because Julia had been willing to explain the consequences. This dating issue was no different than any other lesson of life.

Julia had tried to force back Kelly's natural curiosity about boys by simply telling her no. There had been no explanation, no justification, no rationalization. How could she really have expected Kelly to listen to her when she'd offered no open dialogue on the subject?

Julia hadn't made her fear understandable, hadn't offered any consequences. It was no wonder Kelly had rebelled so strongly against her mother's unexplained rules.

"Mom?"

She looked up from her desk and saw Kelly standing at the doorway of her office.

"Hi, honey," she said. "Come on in. I was just going to call you."

Kelly took one small step inside the door. "We need to talk."

It was more than her daughter's tone of voice that alerted Julia that something was wrong. There was a wariness that sharpened Kelly's dark eyes, as though the child was bracing herself for a fight.

"Yes," Julia told her, "we do need to talk."

Kelly's gaze lit with a fleeting curiosity, but whatever was on her mind was powerful enough to override the interest in what her mother might be about to say.

"Sit down, honey," Julia urged.

Holding her position, Kelly reached up and nervously tucked a wayward strand of her hair behind her ear. Suddenly she blurted, "Sheila's having a party. A big party. With boys. This coming Saturday night. And I want to go."

The calmness that overtook Julia was surprising. Just a few weeks ago she knew she would have lambasted her daughter for even making such a suggestion. She'd have relegated Kelly to her room with no further discussion on the matter.

But now the full picture was clear. Julia knew what needed to be done. Kelly must be made to understand her mother's feelings and fears regarding her daughter's adolescent maturity, and there was only one way to accomplish that.

"Please, Kelly," she said softly, "sit down so we can talk."

The teen narrowed her eyes at her mother, cocking her head the tiniest fraction, as if she couldn't believe her ears. She'd been so ready for an instant denial, or at least an immediate argument.

Kelly moved farther into the room and perched herself on the very edge of the straight-backed chair.

"Before we talk about Sheila's party," Julia said, "I have something I need to tell you."

Julia started out by telling her daughter how much they were alike; strong-willed, confident, outspoken, independent.

"Those are good qualities," she told Kelly. "Most of the time. But you also have to be willing to listen to how someone else feels...someone who might know a little bit more about life than you."

Kelly looked completely baffled, as if she had no clue what point was being made, but Julia plowed ahead.

"I want to tell you a story," she said. She paused a moment. "It's a story that I hope will help you to understand how I feel about you, about you growing older and taking an interest in boys. It's my story, Kelly. I want to tell you my story."

And she did. Julia related her own rebellious behavior as a young woman. Her voice was low, almost whispery soft, as she spoke of the young man who was Kelly's father. Julia didn't give the child all the minute details, but she thought it important that Kelly know how alone and afraid her mother had felt when she discovered she was pregnant and had no one to turn to, nowhere to go.

"My father," she said softly, "was too ill to take care of us. So I left home."

Julia didn't dare tell Kelly about the choice she was

pressured to make; putting her child up for adoption and having a roof over her head, or keeping her baby and suffering complete alienation. The deep-seated bitterness she harbored against Kelly's father and grandfather had nearly ruined her life for the past fifteen years, and Julia didn't want that for her daughter.

"Gosh, Mom," Kelly finally said, "no wonder you never wanted to talk about my dad, or my grandparents."

"What?" A frown bit deeply into her brow. "What are you talking about?"

"Remember when I was little?" her daughter asked. "And my Brownie troop had that father-daughter banquet? You took me shopping instead. We went to a fancy restaurant, and I had lobster for the first time. I still remember that."

Kelly grinned. "And that time in third grade, when the school invited all the grandparents to have lunch with the students, you kept me home for the day. We went to a movie and out for ice cream. It was great."

Julia had forgotten about both incidences. She'd only been trying to protect Kelly, but is seemed her daughter understood her motives just fine. Her smile was soft and loving.

Reaching up and tucking back that same lock of hair, Kelly said, "My dad sounds like he was a real winner."

"He wasn't a bad person, honey," Julia said. "He was just…" Suddenly Ryan's description came to mind. "Immature. Your dad made the worst mistake of his life when he, ah, turned his back on me."

Keeping the emphasis on her rejection was best, Julia thought. She didn't want Kelly feeling deserted.

"Well, he obviously didn't want me, either," Kelly observed.

Unable to change the harsh facts, Julia chose to focus on the positive. "*I* wanted you. From the first moment I knew you were growing inside me. I loved you, and wanted you."

Her words seemed to comfort Kelly a little, but then a shadow crossed over the child's features.

"My grandfather must not have wanted anything to do with me, either," Kelly said. "There's more there than you're telling. I know you, Mom. You wouldn't walk away from your father when he was sick. Not unless you were forced to."

Julia was astounded by her young daughter's perception. Should she lie? she wondered. Should she fabricate some reason why she left home? A reason that would put her father in a better light?

No, she thought. She wouldn't do that. Yet neither did she need to be too explicit.

"All I can tell you, Kelly, is that people make bad choices in life. Choices that can change their lives. And that kind of brings the story full circle."

Julia's gaze intensified. What she was about to say was very important and she wanted her daughter to fully understand.

"I made choices when I was a teenager," she said. "Choices that changed my life. You are the greatest blessing I'll ever have, and I wouldn't change that for the world. But my life was hard, Kelly. I want you to have it easier. I want you to do things the right way."

Kelly blinked once, slowly. And then again. Suddenly her eyes narrowed.

"You're talking about sex, aren't you?" she asked. "You don't want me to have sex."

Sitting stock-still at her desk, Julia froze. She hadn't

expected Kelly to break down the conversation to the very bottom line like this.

"Gee, Mom," she said, "I'd hoped Tyler might kiss me one of these days. But if he ever put his hands on me, I'd have to punch his lights out."

Julia pressed her fingertips to her lips to keep from chuckling. The thought ran through her mind to lecture her daughter against physical violence. However, if Kelly ever felt she was being touched inappropriately, maybe a sock in the nose would be a good deterrent to the perpetrator.

She shook her head, an affectionate gleam in her eyes. "You are something else, Kelly." Then she added, "You have a handle on this boy-girl issue. More than I ever gave you credit for."

Kelly shrugged. "We never really talked about it before."

"I know," Julia admitted. "That was my fault." She widened her eyes and let one corner of her mouth cock upward. "What can I say? Just chalk it up to a loving mother's paranoia."

After a moment Julia said, "Now, about this party of Sheila's...."

In an instant the wariness and fight was back in her daughter's gaze. But it was softened now, softened with a new understanding.

"You've obviously learned from your past mistakes. I know that because you came to me about the party. You even told me the worst part—"

"You mean the part about the *boys?*" Kelly couldn't stop her runaway smile.

"Exactly." Julia couldn't keep from chuckling, either. "You've shown me something. You've shown me that you're growing into a mature young lady."

"Aw, Mom."

She didn't laugh, even though she wanted to. "I mean it, Kelly," she said. "I'm proud of you. And I feel that I can trust you. So I guess you can go to Sheila's Saturday night. Oh, ah, Sheila's parents will be there, won't they?"

"Yes, mother," Kelly said, rolling her eyes.

Shrugging her shoulders, Julia absently reached out and picked up a pencil. "I'm a mom. I'm never going to stop wanting to protect you."

"I know," Kelly whispered. "That kinda makes me feel safe." Then her eyes went wide, as if she just realized what she'd said. "But if you ever tell Sheila I said that, I'll deny it with my dying breath."

Julia sighed, her heart nearly exploding with the love she felt for this child. "You know, Kelly," she said, "you really are the greatest blessing in my life. I'm so grateful to Ryan for making me see that."

It was then that Kelly got up and came around the desk. She put her hand on her mom's arm.

"I don't know what happened between you two," Kelly said. "I know he hasn't come around for a few days. He hasn't called. I know it's really none of my business if you guys broke up. But I gotta tell you, I think he was good for you."

Kelly hugged her then. Tight. And it's just what Julia needed.

She wasn't able to respond. The words couldn't get around the huge lump of emotion that had risen in her throat. Conflicting emotions she easily recognized as happiness and sadness.

Julia felt happy about her talk with Kelly. She felt happy that this young woman she'd previously only

thought of as her daughter was quickly becoming something else—her friend.

And she was sad about what she wouldn't be sharing
with Ryan. A life filled with intimate love and affection.
She was also sad because she agreed with Kelly. Ryan
had been good for her. He'd made her feel wonderful
things she'd never felt before.

But for love to work, the emotion needed to be felt
by *two* people, not just one.

The moon was high and fat, casting bright light
against the dark asphalt as Julia parked her car outside
her house late Saturday night. She was dead tired and
her feet hurt. The dinner party she and Charlotte had
catered had been their largest ever. The profit from the
evening would give both partners of Gold Ribbon Catering a nice bonus. But for some reason, even that
wasn't enough to bring a smile to her face.

What the devil was wrong with her? she wondered as
she sat there in the darkness, listening to the quiet.

Her business was thriving. Her relationship with Kelly
was the best it had ever been. Why wasn't she happy?

Shaking her head, she knew the answer to that question before she could even ask it.

Ryan.

She missed him. Terribly. Missed talking with him.
Missed sharing life's ups and downs with him.

Even though their relationship had been feigned, she'd
been happier than ever while she'd been involved with
him. He'd made her *feel*. He'd made her angry. He'd
made her glad. She'd laughed with him, argued with
him, flirted with him. Ryan had made her feel so alive.
And she'd discovered that was such a nice thing to feel.

Before getting involved in their deal, Julia had been

certain the part of her brain that produced intimate emotions had withered away to nothing. Ryan had proved that idea to be wrong.

She sighed, combing her fingers through her hair. The night was so calm. So quiet. She wished she could somehow tap into that. Somehow displace the aching loneliness she was feeling inside.

Why, oh, why, had she allowed her feeling for Ryan to get out of control?

One corner of her mouth quirked upward ironically. What on earth made her think she could have ever controlled her emotions where Ryan was concerned?

Other forlorn questions floated through her mind, unbidden. Why couldn't happily-ever-after happen in real life? To real people? Why did happy endings only happen between the pages of books?

Julia got out of the car, glanced up at the dark windows of the house and then down at her watch. Kelly didn't need to be picked up at Sheila's for another hour. Plenty of time for a nice, long soak in a scented tub. She grinned suddenly, knowing she meant full well to pull out one of her beloved romance novels. A good, lusty encounter between a fictitious man and a wonton woman was just what she needed, and knowing for certain a happy ending awaited her was just icing on the cake.

She went up the porch steps, sorting among the keys on her ring for the one that would unlock the front door.

"Julia?"

Jumping nearly out of her skin, she backed up a step, her eyes opening wide.

"Ryan," she said, feeling heart-poundingly breathless. "You frightened the life out of me." But in reality, that statement was only a half-truth. Yes, her heart was pounding. Yes, she was breathless. But she'd only experienced a split second of fear. A purely spontaneous reaction, really, to his calling her name when she wasn't expecting it. What had her blood pulsing so furiously was simply the sight of him.

He was sitting on the wicker settee that was positioned at the far end of Julia's small porch.

"I'm sorry," he said. "I tried not to make any sudden moves. I knew whatever I did was going to scare you."

He looked so grieved that Julia couldn't help but assure him. "It's okay." She paused. "Ryan, what are you doing here?"

"I phoned Charlotte today."

"Oh? Didn't she tell you we had a job tonight?"

"Yes," he said. "She did tell me you'd probably be working late." He shrugged. "But there were some things she said, things that had me feeling the need to come see you."

"Oh?" She repeated the tiny word, feeling witless that she couldn't come up with something better to say.

He nodded. "Charlotte said that this evening's party was sort of a coup for Gold Ribbon. I wanted to congratulate you. On the success, I mean."

"Oh, well, thank you." There was a halting quality to her voice. It made her sound almost insincere. The confusion she was feeling was causing it, she knew. There had to be some other reason for Ryan's presence other than the fact that he wanted to congratulate her on a job well done.

She stared at him, wondering what had really prompted him to wait for her in the dark on her porch. Quickly though, the speculation eased away and she found herself drinking in the sight of him.

His tawny head of hair, his lean, handsome face, his blue, blue gaze. She let her eyes feast.

The silence of the night was broken by the barking of a dog over on the next block, and Julia blinked slowly as if she was coming out of some sleepy trance. Ryan must think she was an idiot that she would stand here just staring at him.

Finding her tongue, she asked, "You want to come in for some coffee?"

"Ah, no," he said. "Actually, I'd like to just sit out here, if you don't mind? It's a beautiful night. Would you join me?"

A moment of panic flared up in her chest. She didn't know if she could handle this. Being alone with him. She didn't want to end up making a complete and utter fool of herself.

"Ryan, why are you…" She let the rest of the question fade, realizing that she'd already asked it once.

"Please," he said, "come sit down."

His request was soft and it seemed to put Julia in some sort of strange hypnotic stupor. She moved to the settee and sat down next to him.

She couldn't fight the urge to close her eyes and inhale the warm male scent of him deep into her lungs like the aroma was solid sustenance and she was starved. Exhaling shakily, she fluttered her eyes open and steadied herself, determined not to look like an uncontrollable nitwit.

"Charlotte also told me," Ryan said, breaking the silence, "that you and Kelly have kind of compromised where her boyfriend is concerned. Kelly's at a party tonight with Trevor?"

"Tyler," Julia corrected. Inadvertently, her shoulders

stiffened. "Kelly's attending an *adult-supervised* party, yes."

Ryan smiled and Julia's pulse pounded furiously.

"So you *have* compromised," he observed. His gaze softened as he added, "But I can tell you're still not comfortable with the idea."

She tossed him a look. "Is any mother ever comfortable knowing her daughter's fraternizing with the opposite sex?"

He chuckled at her remark, the sound of it rich and smooth as chocolate cream to Julia's ears. Sheesh, this visit from Ryan was certainly going to be pure torture for her—pure *sweet* torture.

"I did have a plan for Kelly. Where dating was concerned, I mean," Julia said. "I'd thought about it long and hard. Ever since she was just a little girl, I'd planned."

"I guess you did, knowing what you went through as a teenager."

"I was going to let her start dating at sixteen," Julia went on. She shrugged. "I guess I hadn't really taken into consideration the fact that children develop differently. They mature at different ages. I couldn't very well hold her back, and hold her back, and then one day just let her loose." Her tone softened. "That would have been a recipe for disaster."

He nodded. "You're probably right."

Lifting one shoulder, she continued, "So I changed my plan. I decided that, since her interest in boys was a gradual thing, then her exposure to them should be gradual, as well."

She looked up at him, feeling the need to tell the honest truth. "That change of plan is all because of you, you know."

A small, bewildered frown bit into his brow.

Julia shook her head up and down. "You made me look at what I went through. And in reliving my past, I was able to see the future. I didn't want to alienate my daughter. I didn't want to lose her. So I decided to make some concessions. And I think it's a healthy compromise."

"Me, too."

They sat there next to one another, the night quiet creeping up on them again.

He inhaled, as if he was bracing himself for something, and the action drew every nuance of Julia's attention.

"I've been wanting to come see you," he said. Then he hesitated. "The last time we were together…"

Her face flamed and she averted her gaze.

"Julia." He gently captured her chin between his fingers and forced her to look at him. "You said something that bothered me. Something disturbing. Something you need to be set straight on."

She searched his eyes, wondering what it was he was talking about.

He took his hand away from her face. "I haven't come before now because, well, because I've been busy moving and things at the office have been hectic."

"Charlotte told me."

A disgusted sigh passed his lips. "Hell, Julia, that's not the truth."

His sudden loud tone had her spine straightening with surprise.

"The truth is, I haven't come because I felt you needed time away from me."

The wrinkle on his brow bit deeper.

"I was an ass the other night, Julia, and I hope like hell you can forgive me."

Forgive him? Julia pursed her lips. *Forgive him for what? Taking advantage of what she'd so freely offered?*

Before she had a chance to voice the silent questions, he continued.

"I know you probably need more time than what I've given you," he said, "but I just have to talk to you about what you said. It's eating away at me."

"What?" she blurted, unable to stand the suspense any longer. "What did I say that's bothering you so?"

He raked his hand through his hair and then rested his arm across the back of the seat. "You really don't believe that you caused your father to have a stroke, do you? I mean, that's a terrible guilt for a person to be carrying around."

"He had a spell," she said, her voice sounding suddenly frail. She would never have imagined that *this* was what Ryan wanted to discuss, and the surprise had her feeling more than a little shaky. "Right there in my room during our fight."

Ryan's head shook back and forth. "I called a doctor friend of mine. She said your father must have had some kind of predisposing condition. He must have had high blood pressure. Or he smoked. Or something. Discovering you sneaking into the house wasn't something that could trigger a stroke, Julia. Shocking news can't bring one on, either." He grinned despite the somber subject. "My friend says that only happens on television."

She couldn't believe he'd been so worried about that one small statement she'd made. It had bothered him to the point that he'd called a doctor to find out more about what caused people to have strokes.

"I don't want you to carry that guilt around anymore," Ryan told her. "Maybe sneaking out of the house wasn't a good thing for you to do. But you were young. You were a strong-willed teenager who felt she had no other option. And I'm sure the fight you had with your father was unpleasant. But it wasn't enough to cause his illness." He reached out and captured a lock of her short, wavy hair between his index finger and thumb. "It's important to me that you know that."

Why? she wondered, the tiniest light of hope sparking to life inside of her. *Why was it important to him?*

The utter earnestness of his expression was endearing, and she thought it was sweet that he wanted to save her from feeling guilty about her father. She'd held on to that dark emotion for so long, though. Would she be able to let it go?

The back of his thumb brushed her cheek. The contact was accidental, but it made tremors course across her skin just the same. She had to force herself not to lean into his touch.

Why, oh, why, had she fallen so deeply, so completely, for this man? Being near him now was pure agony. An agony she wouldn't have missed for anything!

"There's something else that's been bothering me."

His voice was as intoxicating as dark, rich brandy, and Julia found herself wanting desperately to guzzle enough of it to become mind-numbingly drunk.

"What's that?" she asked, immediately stunned by the sultriness of the two small words as they tumbled from her throat.

What was wrong with her? She had to stop this.

Looking up at his face illuminated by the moonlight, she saw that he hadn't seemed to notice, and she felt relieved.

''The other night,'' he began, ''things between us kind of got...out of hand.''

Heat suffused her cheeks, and although she remained seated, she turned her whole body away frantically. ''It's okay, Ryan. We don't have to talk about that. It's over. It'll never happen again.''

He pressed his palm against her shoulder, the warmth of his skin penetrating the fabric of her blouse.

''I was afraid you'd say that,'' he said.

Regret was evident in his tone. The sound of it confused her, and she swiveled to look at him.

''I made a mistake, Julia. Can't you forgive me?''

His blue eyes were serious, and again she felt bewildered by his question.

''Ryan—''

''No,'' he said, stopping her. ''Hear me out.'' His hand tightened on her shoulder. ''Please.''

She moistened her lips and waited.

''When you told me about your past,'' he said, ''I could see how hurt you were. I could see that you felt betrayed by your father. And by Kelly's father. I could tell you were in such pain. All I wanted was to take it all away. And that's why I kissed you. That's why I...touched you so intimately. I was hoping to whisk you away somewhere safe. Someplace where I could protect you.''

Julia's heart flailed against her chest until she thought sure her ribs could no longer contain its frantic beating. What was he trying to say? Why would he want to protect her? Dear Lord, she hoped he planned to answer her silent questions.

''The mistake I made,'' he continued, ''was in asking you to trust me before making my intentions clear.'' His chin dipped a fraction of an inch. ''You see, I've noticed that you're extremely protective of your emotions. You guard your heart, and your body, fiercely, and I've come to the conclusion that you do that because of what happened to you when you were young.

"You gave Kelly's father your heart," he said. "Your love. You thought your goal and his goal were one and the same. And when you became pregnant, you found out that his intentions weren't what you thought they were."

Julia felt her eyes well with tears. Everything Ryan said was true, and as she thought of her tragic past, sadness washed over her.

"A physical relationship between a man and a woman is a beautiful thing," Ryan told her. "But that alone is a pretty empty feeling."

He cursed under his breath. "I'm making a mess of this. I'm rambling. I should just spit out what I'm trying to say."

Her breath felt caught in her throat, but she forced words across her tongue. "What is it you're trying to say, Ryan? I'd really like to know."

His hand slid down her arm until his palm caressed her bare skin. "I want you to know that my intentions were honorable. I wasn't just looking for a good time. I wanted...I wanted..." He exhaled with force. "It doesn't matter what I wanted because I messed everything up. I messed up any chance we might have had. I messed *us* up."

"Us?" she asked. "There was no us. Ryan, we were pretending to be a couple. There was nothing more between us than that."

"There shouldn't have been, I know." He shook his head. "And I'm really sorry that I..." Again he whispered a curse. "I know I shouldn't have, but I let my feelings for you get away from me."

"What?" Blood pounded through her ears, and she felt woozy and light-headed. "What are you saying?"

"I'm sorry, Julia," he said. "But I've fallen in love with you."

She searched his gaze and then said, "Don't apologize for that."

But he didn't seem to understand her meaning. "I can't help but feel," he plowed ahead, "that if I'd been open about my feelings, about my intentions, before I touched you, then maybe we could have…" He let the rest of the sentence trail.

Julia remembered feeling that something had been missing that night. Something that had her feeling empty. Something that had her desperate to escape. And now she realized what that something was. Ryan's intentions. His feelings. Stated out loud, clear and definite. Well, now she had that.

She laughed. It wasn't a huge, boisterous sound, but it was filled with enough overwhelming joy to make him narrow his eyes at her.

"I can't believe this," she said, her mouth widening with a broad smile.

There were questions in his clear, blue eyes.

"Ryan." She chuckled again, unable to stop the happiness from bubbling up inside her. "I let my feelings get in the way of our deal, too."

He looked suddenly anxious, as if he needed her to be more specific because he didn't believe what he was hearing.

She nodded slowly in the darkness. "I love you, too, Ryan. I love you, too."

Sweeping her up tight against him, he whispered her

name and then planted tiny, grateful kisses on her neck and ear. The light touch of his lips on her skin tickled and she laughed.

He pulled back, a dark trepidation shadowing his gaze. ''What about Kelly?'' he asked. ''How's she going to feel about this? About us?''

She slid onto his lap. ''We'll work it out. Don't worry. She'll be happy for us once she sees how happy we are. She won't be able to help it.''

Cupping her hand against his smooth jaw, she kissed him. Sweetly, gently, she showed him the depth of her intimate feelings, and he showed her his. Her heart swelled with love, and she knew that from this moment on she would never be alone again.

Epilogue

Julia gazed out at the water from the lake's grassy bank and watched as her daughter cast out the fishing line. The elderly man sitting in the rowboat with Kelly nodded and smiled just like the doting grandfather he was. His comment resonated across the still surface of the water, and although Julia couldn't quite make out his exact words, there was no denying the complete approval and pride in his tone. Love and happiness knotted in Julia's chest until it was actually a dull ache.

Setting the romance novel she'd been reading on the grass beside her chair, Julia smiled over at Ryan. "I feel so good," she told him. "No," she corrected, "I feel wonderful."

She reached out and entwined her fingers with his, her diamond wedding ring sliding a fraction to the side. Her gaze automatically darted a quick look at the glittering stone, not yet used to its presence on her hand.

"I can't believe that just a few months ago I was

single,'' she said. ''And fatherless. Well, look at me now. I've got it all.''

Ryan chuckled. ''You deserve it all, Julia.''

After a moment of watching daughter and grandfather out on the lake, Julia asked Ryan, ''Have I thanked you for talking me into calling my dad?''

''Oh, only about two dozen times.''

Her sigh communicated all the contentment she was feeling. ''He's changed so much.''

''Time does that to people,'' Ryan said. ''They mellow with age.''

Julia sat in silence, remembering her father's tears when they'd met for the first time in fifteen years. He'd apologized to her, over and over, for not being the father he should have been, and he couldn't seem to keep his arms from enveloping her and Kelly. Even now, on their fourth visit north to see him, Lester Jones still took every opportunity to lovingly stroke his daughter's cheek, to touch his granddaughter's shoulder or hold her hand. He was trying desperately to make up for all the lost time they'd missed being together.

Ryan and Lester had become fast friends, and for that Julia was grateful. Her husband didn't mind making the two hour trip into Pennsylvania to visit his father-in-law as often as Julia's thriving catering business would allow.

''It would be nice if we could get Dad to come to Wilmington again,'' Julia said. ''I didn't get a chance to show him the city the last time he visited us.''

Lester's one and only trip south had been to walk his daughter down the aisle of the small chapel on her wedding day.

''Let's invite him to come for a visit,'' Ryan suggested. ''I'm sure he'd jump at the chance to spend extra time with Kelly. We could ask him tonight over dinner—''

''Oh, but I was saving some special news for dinner.'' She looked at him coyly, hoping he would nibble at her baited statement.

He grew utterly still. ''Special news?''

One corner of her mouth quirked upward, and she had to work hard to maintain her outward calm when the excitement was getting the best of her. ''Mmm-hmm,'' she said. ''But you know, I probably should tell you before I break the news to Dad and Kelly. I mean, you *did* have a hand in this.'' She grinned like the cat who had caught the canary, refusing to reveal her secret just yet.

''All right, woman,'' Ryan growled. He came out of the aluminum lawn chair, tugging her to her feet, too, and then he led her toward the thick copse of trees that were aflame in autumn color.

Julia laughed, delighted to have gotten such a reaction from the man she loved with all her heart. She didn't mind having to run to keep up with him.

He stopped underneath the scarlet leaves of a huge maple tree, hugging her up against him.

''Okay,'' he whispered against her ear, his sexy voice sending shivers down her spine.

She'd kept this to herself for nearly twenty-four hours, but it was time to share her news—now that she was sure—with the man who had vowed to love her for the rest of her life.

''How would you feel,'' Julia began, feeling suddenly shy and unsure, ''about becoming a daddy?''

Time seemed to stop for them. He didn't speak, didn't even breathe for the length of several heartbeats. He simply looked at her with eyes filled with awe and wonder.

Finally he said, "You mean it? You're sure?"

She nodded.

He gently cupped her face in his hands. "Oh, my..."

Julia had to smile. It was rare that her lawyer husband was at a loss for words.

Ryan kissed the tip of her nose and she felt a heated warmth spread through her.

A shadowy doubt clouded her head and she asked, "Kelly's been an only child for a long time. How do you think she'll take the news?"

His gaze darted out toward the lake. "Are you kidding me?" He smiled down into Julia's face. "She'll be so excited. She's been begging me for a baby brother since you and I got back from our honeymoon."

Julia's furrowed brow smoothed. "I didn't know that." Then she whispered, "Sheesh, that makes me feel so much better. I've been worried."

"Well, don't," he told her, hugging her tight.

Pressing her cheek against his chest, she closed her eyes. "I never thought I'd have the opportunity to have another child. I can't help but feel a little scared. I want to be a good mother for our baby."

"Oh, come on," he lovingly admonished. "You're a great mom. Just look at Kelly. She's quite a young lady."

Without even opening her eyes, Julia smiled. "She is, isn't she?"

They shared this quiet moment together.

Then she looked up at him. "You have to keep this between us until dinner. Promise?"

"But that's nearly four hours away."

His expression told her what she was asking was an impossible task.

"You can do it." She snuggled against him as he

leaned against the sturdy tree trunk. There was nothing that brought two people closer than when they shared an intimate secret.

"You know," he said, "I hope she looks just like you."

"And I hope he looks just like you."

Placing his fingertips under her chin, he lifted her gaze to his. "Hey...what are the chances that we could have twins?"

She shot him a mock glare.

"Or triplets?" he asked.

This time she had to laugh. She loved this man, and with him by her side she could conquer the world. And a hoard of children. Julia was overjoyed to be having a happy ending of her own.

*　*　*　*　*

Look for the next book in Donna Clayton's heartwarming MOTHER & CHILD series. Don't miss WHO'S THE FATHER OF JENNY'S BABY? available in June from Silhouette Romance.

Return to the Towers!

In March
New York Times bestselling author

NORA ROBERTS

brings us to the Calhouns' fabulous
Maine coast mansion and reveals the
tragic secrets hidden there for generations.

For all his degrees, Professor Max Quartermain has a
lot to learn about love—and luscious Lilah Calhoun is
just the woman to teach him. Ex-cop Holt Bradford is
as prickly as a thornbush—until Suzanna Calhoun's
special touch makes love blossom in his heart.
And all of them are caught in the race to solve
the generations-old mystery of a priceless
lost necklace…and a timeless love.

Lilah and Suzanna
THE
Calhoun Women

A special 2-in-1 edition containing
FOR THE LOVE OF LILAH and
SUZANNA'S SURRENDER

Available at your favorite retail outlet.

Take 4 bestselling love stories FREE

a FREE surprise gift!

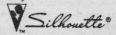

MONTANA Mavericks™

RETURN TO WHITEHORN

Silhouette's beloved **MONTANA MAVERICKS** returns with brand-new stories from your favorite authors! Welcome back to Whitehorn, Montana—a place where rich tales of passion and adventure are unfolding under the Big Sky. The new generation of Mavericks will leave you breathless!

Coming from Silhouette Special Edition®:

February 98: LETTER TO A LONESOME COWBOY by Jackie Merritt

March 98: WIFE MOST WANTED by Joan Elliott Pickart

May 98: A FATHER'S VOW by Myrna Temte

June 98: A HERO'S HOMECOMING by Laurie Paige

And don't miss these two very special additions to the Montana Mavericks saga:

MONTANA MAVERICKS WEDDINGS
by Diana Palmer, Ann Major and Susan Mallery
Short story collection available April 98

WILD WEST WIFE by Susan Mallery
Harlequin Historicals available July 98

Round up these great new stories
at your favorite retail outlet.

V Silhouette®   Look us up on-line at: http://www.romance.net

ALICIA SCOTT

**Continues the
twelve-book series—
36 Hours—in March 1998
with Book Nine**

PARTNERS IN CRIME

The storm was over, and Detective Jack Stryker finally had a
prime suspect in Grand Springs' high-profile murder case. But
beautiful Josie Reynolds wasn't about to admit to the crime—
nor did Jack want her to. He believed in her innocence, and he
teamed up with the alluring suspect to prove it. But was he
playing it by the book—or merely blinded by love?

For Jack and Josie and *all* the residents of Grand Springs,
Colorado, the storm-induced blackout was just the beginning of
36 Hours that changed *everything!* You won't want to miss a
single book.

Available at your favorite retail outlet.

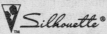

DIANA PALMER
ANN MAJOR
SUSAN MALLERY

MONTANA MAVERICKS *Weddings*

RETURN TO WHITEHORN

In **April 1998** get ready to catch the bouquet. Join in the excitement as these bestselling authors lead us down the aisle with three heartwarming tales of love and matrimony in Big Sky country.

A very engaged lady is having second thoughts about her intended; a pregnant librarian is wooed by the town bad boy; a cowgirl meets up with her first love. Which Maverick will be the next one to get hitched?

Available in **April 1998**.

Silhouette's beloved **MONTANA MAVERICKS** returns in Special Edition and Harlequin Historicals starting in February 1998, with brand-new stories from your favorite authors.

Round up these great new stories at your favorite retail outlet.

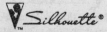